E7t

2 8 SEP 2021

D1744841

SAY YES

Harrison Kincaid's mother wants to fix him up with a wife, but he has no intention of falling for any woman chosen by her . . . until he sees the gorgeous Amanda Whitfield. Amanda thinks Harrison has potential and agrees to let him escort her to her cousin's upcoming wedding — after he's had a complete makeover. When Harrison obliges and steps out of the dressing room, Amanda sees that clothes really do make the man. Could she be falling in love . . . ?

Books by Joan Reeves
in the Linford Romance Library:

LOVE WILL FIND A WAY
MOST WANTED

JOAN REEVES

SAY YES

Complete and Unabridged

LINFORD
Leicester

First published in the
United States of America in 2000

First Linford Edition
published 2009

British Library CIP Data

Reeves, Joan
    Say yes.—Large print ed.—
    Linford romance library
    1. Love stories
    2. Large type books
    I. Title
    823.9′2 [F]

    ISBN 978–1–84782–530–8

Published by
F. A. Thorpe (Publishing)
Anstey, Leicestershire
Set by Words & Graphics Ltd.
Anstey, Leicestershire
Printed and bound in Great Britain by
T. J. International Ltd., Padstow, Cornwall

For Melanie Christine Reeves Hutzler. You are beautiful, tenderhearted, and compassionate. Your picture should be next to the word wonderful *in the dictionary.*

And, as always, thanks for the memories, L.A.R.

1

Amanda Whitfield needed a man. Desperately. But where was she going to find one in time for Valentine's Day? Manhunting, even in a city the size of Houston, had proved unsuccessful. She had nothing to show for her efforts — not to mention the efforts of her best friend Nicole Patrick, who had also drawn a blank.

Frowning, Amanda stirred the bowl of black walnut ice cream. Usually she adored the unusual flavor, but she might as well have been eating plain old vanilla for all the notice she took. Even the lovely tearoom with its lace-covered tables and rose-velvet cushioned chairs failed to captivate her today.

'Geez, Louise, Amanda! If your favorite ice cream won't cheer you up, then what will?' Nicole's question seemed abnormally loud against the backdrop of quiet conversation and melodic harp music which poured from hidden speakers.

'How about a date for Marcy's wedding?' Amanda's expression looked as doleful as she sounded.

'I don't understand why you're even going to your snooty cousin's wedding. Marcy is the type who gives smart women a bad name. Just because her IQ is recorded in some intellectual hall of fame doesn't make her someone to hang with. So why go?'

'You know why.' Amanda looked at the unappealing mush of melted ice cream and shoved the bowl away. 'Everyone in the family will talk if I don't go.'

'Let them talk.' Nicole laughed. 'Better yet, tell your mom to dig you up a date.'

Amanda shuddered. 'No, thank you. The last time I let her do that was when she fixed me up with one of Dad's golf partners.'

Nicole covered her grin with both

hands. 'You mean Buddy? That nice white-haired gentleman?'

'Sure, go ahead and laugh. Some friend you are.'

'Hey, I'm a great friend. Who else would double-date on a moment's notice?' She choked back a laugh. 'Come on. You've got to admit it was pretty funny. As I remember it, there may have been snow on his roof, but his fire definitely wasn't out.'

'Yeah, if ever a guy needed a bucket of cold water, it was Buddy.' Just recalling her last date months ago deepened Amanda's gloom. 'Mom's desperate. That's why she's beating the bushes for any male under sixty.'

'Yeah, my mom's the same way — convinced I'll be an old maid if I haven't got a man hog-tied before my thirtieth birthday.'

'Then we only have two years to go, Nicole.' Amanda's fingers plucked at a whorl in the lace tablecloth. 'What's wrong with me, anyway?' She was completely frustrated with her non-existent love life. Just as the music faded, she asked, an edge of desperation to her voice, 'Why can't I get a date?'

The question dropped like a boulder into a quiet pool of water. Hot color flooded Amanda's fair complexion. She glanced around quickly, hoping everyone was engrossed in their own conversations and hadn't heard her plaintive question.

Two women of her mother's age, at the table on her right, stared back. The woman with short brown hair — wearing one of Amanda's favorite scents, Youth Dew — quickly dropped her gaze to her salad, but her lunch partner, who wore Chanel No. 5, smiled at Amanda. Her expression conveyed such sympathy that Amanda felt even worse.

As a perfume designer, it was nearly impossible for Amanda to notice anyone without noting what fragrance they wore. She supposed it was an occupational hazard. Right now, she didn't want to notice or to be noticed.

'Great. Now everyone can talk about

the loser at table three,' she grumbled.

Nicole patted her hand. 'If they're talking, it's because they're amazed that a woman who looks like you has a problem getting a man. You probably made their day!' She grinned. 'And to answer your question, there's nothing wrong with you. You're smart. You're funny. You're beautiful. You — we — own a business that's fabulous. Face it, kid. You're perfect.'

Amanda rolled her eyes. 'Gee, thanks for explaining it to me. That clears up the mystery for sure. So you're saying that men want dumb, serious, ugly women? How could I not know that?'

'Amanda, men take one look at those big blue eyes and that long blonde hair' — she waved her hands up and down — 'and that body, and they figure you have men on a waiting list the size of the Houston phone book. Or they think you wouldn't give them the time of day because they aren't your equal in looks.'

'What do they think? That I only want to date Val Kilmer, Brad Pitt, or

Pierce Brosnan?'

'Those guys are taken, honey.'

'So that makes my possible dating pool even smaller.'

Nicole shrugged. 'Men don't like being rejected. They look at you and figure you'll shoot them down the minute they try.'

'But I wouldn't reject a guy just because of his looks.'

'Oh, come on. You're just like me and every other woman out there. You want a tall, dark, handsome millionaire to sweep you off your feet.'

Amanda shook her head. 'You're wrong. I'd go out with any man who would ask me, but no one ever does — at least, not after the first date. I seem to have the unique ability to meet men who fall into instant *like* with me.'

'Maybe it's because — ' Nicole stopped. Her gaze dropped.

'Because why?' Amanda studied her friend. 'What were you going to say?'

Nicole took a deep breath. 'It's because you put out these vibes that say you're interested in being friends, not lovers. You hardly even notice men except when there's an occasion you need an escort for. Then you get in a panic to find a man.'

'That's not true!' Amanda stared incredulously at her friend.

'Yes, it is. Men don't like to be ignored. You've got this invisible Do Not Disturb sign hanging around your neck.'

'Well . . . well, then I'll . . . I'll switch it off.'

'How if you're not even aware of it?'

Amanda frowned. 'There might be some truth to what you said. Maybe it's because I've never really met any man who interested me enough to even think about a relationship beyond friendship.'

Nicole said, 'Could be. Then there's the problem of the remaining men.'

'The remaining men? You make them sound like the survivors of a nuclear holocaust,' Amanda grumbled.

Nicole laughed. 'The ones who aren't

intimidated, and who haven't become your best bud, buy into the blonde myth.'

'Which myth is that? That blondes are bubbleheads-with-a-bra-size-larger-than-their-IQ myth or that blondes-are-nymphomaniacs myth?' Amanda asked sourly.

Nicole grinned. 'The bubblehead myth. I hadn't considered the nympho myth. Blondes do have a rep for being brainless.'

'You're telling me? If I get any more blonde jokes by e-mail from my darling cousin Marcy, I'm going to spam her e-mail box with lawyer jokes until she can't open it.'

'What's the difference between a dead snake and a dead lawyer, both lying in the middle of a road?' Nicole asked, humor sparkling in her green eyes.

Laughter from the other table drew Amanda's attention. An older woman with friendly brown eyes said, 'There's skid marks in front of the dead snake.'

She and her friend giggled like two high school girls. She shrugged. 'My father and my husband both were lawyers. I know every lawyer joke out there.'

Amanda chuckled weakly. Her private conversation seemed to have turned into a talk show call-in. 'Come on, Nicole.'

'Yeah, let's get out of here and go somewhere private — like the middle of a crowded mall.' Nicole chuckled and followed.

★ ★ ★

'What do you think?' Lynn Kincaid asked her friend Betty Gonzalez as they watched the two young women pay the restaurant cashier.

'Oh, no! I'm tired of the looks we've been getting from these girls. Won't the blonde we met at the health food store in the mall do?'

Lynn waved her hands to dismiss Betty's comment. 'I never seriously considered *her*. My old sofa has more padding than her bottom. She couldn't possibly give birth without problems.' She pulled cash from her purse and tossed it onto the table.

'What's wrong with the girl we met at the cookie stand?'

'She obviously lives on cookies, Betty. My son has to be able to carry his bride over the threshold. It's a Kincaid tradition. Come on. Let's tail that blonde. She's a fox.'

Her friend rolled her eyes. 'It's bad enough you browbeat me into helping you with this crazy scheme, but do you have to talk like a cheap detective? Besides, I think the term fox is passé now.'

When Lynn ignored her, Betty asked, 'Have I told you there's something a little obsessive about your quest to find a wife for your son?'

'Every time we scope out the prospects.'

'I'm beginning to feel like I'm Ethel Mertz, and you're Lucy Ricardo,' Betty grumbled as she got to her feet.

'Don't worry, Betty, you're too skinny for anyone to ever mistake you for Ethel, and I'm a long way from being a redhead.'

Lynn paused at the door. 'There they are — standing next to that red Corvette.'

'Heck! Why not just go up and say 'Pardon me, miss, but would you like to marry my son and bear his children?''

'Don't be silly. I won't start with a marriage proposal. I'll just begin the usual way by suggesting a date.'

Betty rolled her eyes. 'Do you honestly think any woman will go out on a blind date with a guy whose mother set it up? Get serious. She'd think he was a total loser. Even if you got a girl to say yes, Harrison won't agree to it. Not after last time.'

Lynn frowned. 'I know I've got my work cut out for me, but by golly, I'm determined. I'm tired of waiting for him to settle down. He's not interested in anything except computers and running around. I want grandchildren

11

while I'm young enough to enjoy them. And I don't mean cyber grandchildren.'

'Harrison dates. He never seems to lack for girlfriends.'

'That's the problem,' Lynn said, keeping an eye on Amanda. 'He's got a girl in every cyber port! Why can't he be like your Eddie and settle down? But no, he just wants to have a good time. Well, I'm putting an end to that.'

Betty giggled. 'Did you hear what you just said?'

Lynn grabbed her friend's arm. 'Let's hustle. They're getting into the car.'

'I still say this is crazy,' Betty grumbled as she followed.

'Hush, Betty. This is perfect. You heard that girl. She's desperate for a date, and I'm desperate for my son to get married. This just might be a match made in heaven.'

'Oh, miss? Miss?' Lynn called loudly as she raced toward Amanda, dragging her reluctant friend in her wake. 'May I have a word with you, please?'

2

Harrison Kincaid stared at the perfectly-cooked slab of pot roast on his plate and the mound of mashed potatoes dripping with rich brown gravy. Golden-crusted dinner rolls, hot from the oven, confirmed his suspicions. His dark eyes fixed on his mother who sat across the table from him.

'So, is this the culinary version of 'Come into my parlor, said the spider to the fly?''

'What on earth do you mean?' Lynn sputtered. She met her son's accusing gaze with wide-eyed innocence.

'Who's the girl?' Harrison sighed. Every time his mother went all out to cook him a meal, he knew she had a date lined up for him. Why wouldn't she accept that he was happy with his life?

'Come on, Mom. You lured me here

with the promise of my favorite dinner. Are you going to spring the trap when I'm too stuffed to escape?'

Lynn laughed. 'Eat your dinner. You never get a home-cooked meal unless you come to visit me. You know, I won't be around forever. What will you do for real food after I'm gone?'

Yep. He was in for it. She was packing that big gun of guilt — and she wasn't afraid to use it. He laid his fork down. His appetite nearly vanished at the realization that she must have another of her friend's daughters to pawn off on him. Why was it that all her friends had such singularly unattractive offspring?

'Mom,' he complained, 'I thought after the last blind date you forced me into that we had reached an agreement about this.'

'I didn't know Sherry's daughter had been divorced four times. Or was it her pierced tongue you objected to?' Lynn frowned, then shrugged. 'In any case, you shouldn't hold that against me.

14

This new girl has never been married. She's just as sweet as can be and has an absolutely great personality. And the only thing pierced are her ears,' she added brightly.

Harrison groaned. 'A great personality?' If ever a phrase struck terror into a single man's heart, it was that one — especially when used to describe a blind date.

'Bless her heart. She was so distraught about not having a date for her cousin's wedding. Before I knew what I was doing, I'd promised that you'd escort her. If you just do this little favor for me, I'll never bother you again.'

'That's what you said last time, and the time before. Is she a friend's daughter?' He grinned, amused as he was frustrated.

'Oh, she's my friend. Why, I can't tell you how long we've been friends. Haven't I ever mentioned her before?' Lynn waved her hands. 'We'll talk later. Your food's getting cold.'

Harrison was torn between walking

out in protest or digging into the meal his mother had prepared. She had him at an unfair advantage, and she knew it. In the end, his stomach overruled his common sense. Finally, when he couldn't eat another bite, his mother began clearing the table.

'Let me get the dishwasher started and then I'll serve dessert in the den.' Lynn stacked the dishes.

'Dessert? Mom, I'm stuffed.' Harrison patted his hard mid-section.

'Oh, pooh. As much as you work out, you'll burn it off in the gym tomorrow. Besides, you're a growing boy, Harrison.'

'I'm twenty-nine, remember? I don't think I'm going to grow past the six feet I've already reached. Unless you're talking about growing sideways.'

'You'll never have to worry about getting fat. You've got your father's metabolism.' Lynn's face softened. 'You look so much like him with that black hair and velvety brown eyes. It's like seeing him when he was your age.' She cleared her throat and turned away, silently gathering the soiled napkins.

'You still miss him after all these years, don't you?' Harrison drew her into his arms and hugged her.

Lynn blinked rapidly. 'Yes. I still do. He was the other half of me. I guess that's why I want you to find someone. I know how wonderful it is to share your life with someone.'

Harrison remained silent. His casual approach to dating made perfect sense to him. He swallowed over the knot of emotion in his throat. He still missed his dad, too — though it had been ten years since a heart attack had taken the senior Kincaid.

'Maybe I could force a little dessert down,' he said, wanting to make her smile. 'What did you have in mind?'

Lynn snuffled and pulled away from him. 'Baked Alaska all right with you?' she said, forcing a smile.

'You're kidding, right?' He picked up the stacked plates and carried them to the kitchen.

'Just need to pop it in the oven to brown the meringue.' Lynn patted his cheek. 'Go sit in your dad's recliner and put your feet up. I'll serve dessert, and we'll talk.'

Harrison knew he was a goner. How could a man refuse a favor for a mother who prepared roast beef and gravy and topped it off with Baked Alaska?

He settled into the chair his mother still called his dad's recliner, even though it had been reupholstered twice since his dad had sat in it. He had to make his mother stop this matchmaking.

A half hour later, Lynn had told him all about Amanda Whitfield and her great personality. She served him another chunk of dessert. 'So you'll escort Amanda to her cousin's wedding?'

Harrison, taste buds going wild at a mouthful of meringue-frosted cake and ice cream, nodded. He'd let his mother enjoy what she thought was her triumph. This would be her last attempt at matchmaking. Somehow, he'd put an end to her schemes.

He took another bite of the luscious dessert. Poor Amanda. His mental picture of her wasn't very flattering. Most likely she'd resemble the other desperate women his mother had thrown at him.

'What did you tell this Amanda about me?'

'Oh, that you were a tall, dark, handsome, rich computer genius, with Bill Gates' brains and Antonio Banderas' looks.' Lynn smiled with pride at him. 'But without the sexy accent.'

'Oh, yeah? So she's expecting a smart, good-looking manly man, huh?' His eyes gleamed as a plan began to take shape.

'Exactly! And I kind of promised you'd meet her tomorrow night.'

'You did?' Harrison sighed. 'And exactly where is this blind date supposed to take place?'

Lynn's dark eyes gleamed. 'I thought the nightclub that was written up in the

Sunday's entertainment section would be the perfect place. It's called Retro. It sounded like such a nice place. Good music in a charming setting.'

'If it sounds so nice, why don't you go?'

'Oh, no. I'd feel funny going with you on your date.'

'Mom, I meant go there yourself sometime.'

'By myself?' Lynn looked horrified at the idea.

'No, with a date.'

At that, Lynn's eyes rounded and she looked even more horrified. 'Harrison!'

Harrison looked at his mother as if seeing her for the first time in a long time. She was attractive and still young by today's standards. He'd never thought about it, but why shouldn't she date someone?

'Mom, have you even had a date since Dad died?'

'I think we need to change the subject. We were talking about your love life. Not mine.' Lynn laughed nervously.

'Besides, I'm too old to date. I wouldn't know how to act.'

The wistful note in her voice surprised Harrison. She was lonely, he suddenly realized. No wonder she was trying to provide herself with a daughter-in-law and grandchildren. He knew that his dad wouldn't have wanted her to be lonely.

'Okay, if we're talking about my love life, didn't this Amanda think it was strange for you to set up dates for your son?'

'Not at all,' Lynn sputtered. 'She was grateful.'

Yeah, he bet the poor, desperate old maid was grateful. Maybe she was a librarian with a knot of mousy hair at the nape of her neck like Miss Blue back in elementary school. How that woman had terrified him.

'What time am I supposed to meet her at Retro?'

'Is eight o'clock all right? Amanda's such a lovely girl. I know you'll like her. So sweet and kind.'

'Sweet, kind, great personality! What more could a man want?' Harrison knew exactly what a man wanted in a woman, and it wasn't the mental image he'd formed of Amanda Whitfield.

He'd meet her, but no way would he escort her to a wedding. Women tended to get crazy ideas at weddings. But he didn't tell his mother that. She didn't need to know that any more than she needed to know he planned to put an end to her matchmaking. Which might also put an end to her loneliness.

Two could play this matchmaking game. Yep, what Mom needed was something more in her life. If she had a man, she wouldn't have time to meddle in his affairs. He'd find the perfect man for her, he decided, just as soon as he'd gotten rid of her latest candidate for the position of Mrs. Harrison Kincaid.

By the time he and the undoubtedly homely Amanda finished their first date, Miss Whitfield wouldn't want to go across the street with him, much less to a relative's wedding.

3

Amanda arrived early and parked at the side of Retro, the newest place to hear good music in a setting quiet enough for conversation. Though she had worn a long-sleeved sheath of red wool, she shivered. The chill that snaked its way up her spine couldn't be blamed entirely on the blue norther that had hit Houston while the city slept last night.

Gleaming mahogany double doors opened to a palm-dotted foyer of black and white marble. Her red suede pumps clicked against the foyer's tiles as she walked toward the arched double doorway.

'Amanda. How nice to see you,' said an attractive black woman seated at an antique writing desk to the right of the arch.

'Darla, how are you?' Amanda smiled

warmly. Darla Howard had been one of her first clients.

The woman who guarded the reservations book at her command post said, 'Nicole is at the bar. I wish one of you had called. I'd have saved your favorite table for you.'

'Thanks, but I'm here to meet' — she grimaced — 'a man.'

Darla's eyes widened. 'A man?'

'Don't sound so incredulous.' Amanda laughed ruefully. 'I do occasionally have a date.'

'I apologize.' Darla patted Amanda's shoulder.

'No need. His name is Harrison Kincaid. Would you point him in my direction when he arrives?' At Darla's nod, Amanda said, 'I can't believe I'm doing this — after I swore off blind dates.'

Darla's smile widened. 'I met my husband on a blind date. It was love at first sight. And second. And third. What a guy!'

'Having seen your husband, I agree,'

Amanda said. 'I don't think this date is going to turn out quite like that.'

'If things don't work out with him, stay and listen to Stan. He's in great form tonight.'

'Your brother is always in great form.' Amanda chatted a few minutes more, then excused herself and entered the club. A handful of people were scattered throughout the room, but she didn't see anyone who seemed to be waiting for someone.

The bar, a curving expanse of gleaming mahogany, was crowned by an array of sparkling crystal tumblers and stemmed glasses. Empty red-cushioned bar stools filled the space between a softly cooing couple at one end and Nicole, impatiently tapping her feet on the shiny brass foot rail, at the other.

Amanda slid into the chair next to Nicole and looked around. 'I guess he's not here yet.'

'Couldn't be. These guys look too good to be your date.'

Amanda rolled her eyes. 'Don't start!'

She wiped her perspiring hands on the sides of her dress and surveyed the club. It was the kind of place she imagined must have existed in New York in the forties. She loved its elegant sophistication.

Round clear glass bowls of red roses elegantly accented the starched white linen-covered tables. The wait staff — men in severe black tuxedos with red bow ties and women wearing red satin chokers and black crepe cocktail dresses — moved quietly while Stan played Gershwin tunes on the high-gloss ebony grand piano.

'Thanks for keeping me company, Nicole. I was hesitant to come here after what happened last time.'

'An overly enthusiastic Romeo like Thomas Brighton will be the least of your troubles tonight.' Nicole patted Amanda's hands. 'It's okay though. I'm here to save you. After all, friends don't let friends date ugly men.' She grinned. 'Besides, I wouldn't miss seeing this guy for anything.'

'You're so certain he's a loser?'

'Amanda, any guy who has his mother scouting out dates has to be a major loser. Lynn said,' — Nicole ticked the adjectives off on her fingers — 'tall, dark, handsome, rich, computer genius. That's in motherese. Translated to plain English, tall means he's tall enough to be a center for the Rockets. With your five feet four inches next to him, you'll look like a toddler.'

'Dark? Let me guess,' Amanda said. 'He's got skin that looks like a sunburned lizard.'

'Oh, no. He can't be tanned because he's a computer genius. Those guys are like garden moles. They never see daylight.'

'So what does dark mean?'

'He's covered with hair — even his back. A regular ape man.'

Amanda's lips twitched. 'What about handsome?'

'Oh, that's an outright lie. Mothers are entitled to one good lie when describing their undesirable sons.'

Amanda grinned at Nicole's silliness. 'Computer genius is easy. He's a total geek complete with pocket protector and high water pants.'

'Yep. I can see it now.' Nicole held up both hands as if she were viewing a movie through them. 'It'll be a replay of that classic fairy tale beloved by all — *Beauty and the Geek*.'

Amanda laughed in spite of herself. 'Well, I guess I can look on the bright side. At least he'll be easy to spot.'

Nicole shook her head slowly. 'You really need your head examined. This guy must be more desperate than you.'

'But his mother is attractive! And she wears Chanel.'

'Her choice of perfume doesn't make her son presentable.'

Amanda knew her friend was right. 'Maybe he won't show.'

Nicole laughed. 'You couldn't be that lucky.'

'You can laugh and joke all you want. I don't care what he looks like — despite your opinion. I'm going to smother him with charm. He'll be so besotted that he'll be thrilled to escort me.'

'Whatever you say, though that seems kind of mercenary.'

Uneasy with that observation, Amanda said, 'I'm going to charm him, but I won't lead him on. I'll make sure he sees that Do Not Disturb sign around my neck.'

Nicole snorted. 'That's a fine line I wouldn't want to walk. You know there are worse things than going to this wedding alone.'

'Maybe for you, but all I've ever heard from dear cousin Marcy is how sorry she feels for me, her dumb blonde cousin.'

'Like I said, don't go.'

'If she's said it once, she's said it a thousand times. Looks don't mean as much as brains.' Amanda parroted her cousin in the clipped pseudo-British accent Marcy affected. 'I'm just so thankful that I'm smart rather than beautiful — after all, beauty fades but brains last, dear Amanda.'

'You're not exactly brain dead, Amanda!'

'Oh, I know that.' Amanda ground her teeth. 'Let's just call it one of those stigmas from childhood that I can't shake. What made it worse was that she always had a boyfriend, and I never had one. Fat lot of good my so-called beauty did me.'

Nicole stood. 'Hold that thought. I've got to go to the ladies' room. Order us a couple of martinis. I'll be right back.'

Amanda ordered a martini for Nicole and a club soda with an olive in a martini glass for herself. The drinks arrived before her friend returned.

From the corner of her eye, she saw someone slide onto the next chair. Could it be him? She looked up and met the smirking face of the one man she didn't want to see. He blew a smoke ring at her. Amanda coughed and her spirits sank to a new low.

'Hello, Mr. Brighton. How's your lovely wife?' she asked, her voice as cold as the perfectly chilled martini glass.

'She still doesn't understand me, Amanda. Don't you want to take me to your breast and comfort me?' he asked silkily.

She had to get rid of this jerk before her date arrived. 'The only thing I'd like to do is kick you where your brains obviously are contained,' she said, not bothering to soften her rejection. 'I'm not interested in you.'

Harrison hesitated in the doorway so he could scope out his date. He looked toward where the hostess pointed. There must be a mistake. Amanda Whitfield was supposed to be homely. From what he could see, the blonde wasn't the least bit plain. The man next to her didn't seem to find her unattractive either, and kept trying to talk to her, but she seemed to be ignoring him.

Even through the distortion of the cheap magnifying glasses he'd bought at the drugstore, Harrison easily read her body language. *Get lost*, it said, loud and clear. She wanted nothing to do with the guy. Judging by the two spots of ruddy color in the man's cheeks, she was now giving him a stinging set-down. He shoved away from the bar and left without a backward glance at Amanda Whitfield. Kind? Sweet? Tell that to the guy she just blasted.

Impulsively, Harrison followed Amanda's victim to the men's room. The man was splashing cold water on his face. His eyes met Harrison's in the mirror. He snorted, 'Women! They make you hot one way or the other!'

'I noticed that woman you were talking to at the bar.'

'Kind of hard to miss her, isn't it?' He made a rude sound. 'If you were thinking about trying your luck, I'd forget it.'

'Cold, huh?' Harrison asked.

'She knows she's beautiful and thinks that gives her the right to treat men like dirt. I wouldn't bother her if I were you.' He looked Harrison up and down. 'Especially if I were you.'

* * *

'If that two-faced, philandering jerk makes another heavy-handed pass at me again, Nicole, I think I'll call his wife.' Amanda fanned her heated face with her napkin.

'No, you won't. You know it would hurt Connie to discover the truth about him. She's totally clueless and completely infatuated with the jerk, heaven help her.'

'Someone needs to open her eyes,' Amanda grumbled.

'Don't waste your time worrying about him. You've got bigger problems.' Nicole looked around. 'Any new men?'

'No.' Amanda shuddered. 'Maybe this blind date won't be so bad. After the creepy crawly Brighton, a nice sweet guy will be refreshing, even if he is kind of nerdy.'

Nicole sipped her drink and eyed Amanda's glass. 'You really should cultivate a taste for martinis.'

Amanda grimaced. 'They taste like gasoline.'

'If men only knew how unsophisticated you really are.'

'Maybe that's my problem.' Amanda continued thoughtfully. 'I get a date with a good-looking guy, and he thinks he's going out with somebody hip and cool. Then he finds out I'm just ordinary.'

'You're not ordinary. It's that Do Not Disturb sign.'

'Well, if I ever meet a guy who makes me want to remove that sign, I'm going to be so darned hip and cool and charming that he won't know what hit him,' Amanda grumbled.

'In the meantime, I'll just make do with Harrison Kincaid. If he's really a genius, and as successful as Lynn said, it won't matter what he looks like because people make exceptions for genius or for money. Maybe Marcy would sit up and take notice if I showed up with a genius — regardless of his looks. She was always telling me I could attract a man if I improved my mind.'

Nicole sputtered, 'Give me a break! And you believed that?'

'More so than I realized. It seems to have stuck with me.'

'Did it ever occur to you that the reason Marcy had so many boyfriends is because she was doing the wild thing with them?'

That surprised a laugh out of Amanda. 'Actually, no. It never did. Do you really think so?'

Nicole shrugged. 'Most of the girls I knew in school who were ultra popular had a rep for being free with their favors.'

'Well, that does cast a different light on the whole thing. Nevertheless, I want to show her up, Nicole.'

Nicole's eyebrows rose. 'Show her up? So we've gone from getting a man — any man — to showing her up? How do you intend to do that when she's the blushing bride with the one carat perfect diamond?'

'Well, if Harrison is as wonderful as his mother said — '

'Yeah, what are the odds?' Nicole muttered. 'You really are a dreamer.' She looked away. Her gaze roamed the room then came to an abrupt halt.

Amanda swirled the olive in her martini glass. As if trying to convince herself, she repeated, 'It won't matter what he looks like as long as he's smart and successful. Right?'

When Nicole didn't reply, Amanda shook her. Nicole's eyes were as round as the rim of the martini glass. 'Nicole?'

Her friend picked up her martini and downed the remainder. Then she grabbed Amanda's glass from her hand and gulped it also.

'Amanda,' she gasped, staring across the room, 'for your sake, I hope he's got the IQ of Einstein and more bucks in the bank than Bill Gates. That would be the only reason for going out with Harrison Kincaid.'

Amanda followed Nicole's gaze. Her eyes widened. Her mouth dropped open. She felt the blood drain from her face.

Her blind date had arrived.

4

Harrison figured it should take about five minutes for Amanda to send him packing, judging by what the guy in the bathroom had said. Four minutes for her to recover from the dead faint when she saw him, and one minute to tell him to get lost.

Stunned by the woman who was his blind date, he forgot to hitch up the polyester trousers so they would display his white cotton socks. Instead, he walked slowly toward her as if he were in a trance.

He let the oversized black-framed glasses slide down his nose a bit so he could see where he was going. Looking over the magnifying lenses, he got his first clear look at his mother's latest prospect and nearly tripped over his own feet. He felt as if he'd been sucker-punched.

Amanda Whitfield wasn't just attractive. The woman was the stuff dreams were made of — at least men's dreams. Harrison frowned. This made no sense. Why would a woman who looked like this even agree to a blind date? What was it his mom had said? The woman desperately needed an escort for a relative's wedding?

He didn't believe it. This woman would never have to beg for male company. He had no doubt that men were probably lined up around the block waiting for a smile from her. Something didn't add up.

If there was one thing Harrison Kincaid couldn't walk away from, it was a mystery or a puzzle of any kind.

Watching Amanda's horror-struck expression as he approached, he tried to reconcile what he saw with what he'd been told. It just didn't make sense. He was concentrating so hard that he forgot to slouch as he walked.

Amanda gaped at him. Time seemed to slow just the way it did in cheesy horror films. Her voice held a note of awe. 'Have you ever seen clothes like that before, Nicole?'

'Only on the audiovisual guys back in high school. You know, the ones who showed the filmstrips on pollywogs and fruit fly genetics.'

'No wonder he has to let his mother set up blind dates for him. Too bad she doesn't dress him as well.' Amanda closed her eyes and then opened them again, hoping against hope that her date would magically transform into something approaching acceptable. But he didn't. The closer he got, the worse he seemed. His hair, parted in the middle and plastered to his head, gleamed wetly.

'Nicole, there is no way I can go to Marcy's wedding with this guy! I'd be the laughingstock of the family. Even if my mother didn't kill me for embarrassing her, my cousin Marcy would never let me live it down.'

'I thought you didn't care what he looked like.' Nicole's voice sounded awed. 'Oh, my goodness. He really does have a pocket protector.'

'I'm sunk. This isn't happening.'

'Oh, it's happening all right. Not quite as fast as a train wreck but just as disastrous.'

'When I said I didn't care what he looked like, I didn't know any man could look this bad.' Amanda grimaced. 'It's not like you said. I'm really not looking for a perfect man. Oh, go ahead. Call me shallow. I don't care. Just tell me how I'm going to get out of this?'

'Let him down gently — but swiftly,' Nicole whispered.

'Shhh. Don't say anything else! He'll hear.'

Silently, Amanda and Nicole waited. Then he was next to them. Both women craned their necks upward, gawking in dismay at the vision of bad taste.

'Hello,' Harrison said, forgetting the hokey greeting he'd planned to make. Close up, Amanda was a knock-out!

And her friend wasn't bad either, he thought, sparing a glance for the redhead.

'I'm Harrison Kincaid.'

When Nicole thrust out her hand, he shook it, but his eyes remained on Amanda. Absently, he nodded and murmured something appropriate to the redhead. He didn't hear what she said. His eyes never left Amanda's. He slid into the chair on her left.

'Let me guess. You're Amanda.' He stated, knowing full well who she was.

'Yes. Yes, I am.' She offered her hand, and he eagerly grasped it, wanting to feel the texture of her skin. His hand enclosed hers. Her hand fit perfectly. It felt warm — the skin smooth as silk. His palm seemed to vibrate at her touch.

'Amanda, my pleasure.'

Amanda's eyes widened and dropped to their joined hands, trying to make sense of the riot of sensations his touch elicited. The feel of his skin was like his voice — unexpected.

From the corner of her eye, she saw Nicole frown. She knew what her friend was thinking and agreed. His voice didn't sound like the voice of a guy who would wear orange and brown plaid polyester. And his hand wasn't the limp-wristed grip she expected from a computer geek. And his smell. Oh! Indescribably delicious!

Finding her voice, she said, 'This is my friend Nicole Patrick.'

'I already introduced myself,' Nicole said, amusement in her voice. She looked from Amanda to Harrison. Her frown gradually transformed to a half-smile playing about her lips.

His scent, strange, yet appealing, drifted to Amanda. She frowned, trying to identify its components. Musk, yes, but the rest was more of a fleeting sensation than a smell — something like the way she'd felt when she got her very first kiss in the moonlight. A shiver of awareness raised the fine hairs on her neck. Thoroughly confused at her body's reaction, she stared at him as if his face held the answer.

'Cold?' he asked. He leaned a little closer.

'No. Not at all.' Amanda rubbed her arms in apparent contradiction.

Harrison decided that he'd be glad to keep her warm. She had that 'hands off' look truly beautiful women seemed to have been born with, but that just made him want to caress every inch of her perfect skin. His heart beat faster just imagining what it would be like.

'May I buy you ladies a drink?' Going out with Amanda, even to a wedding, might not be so bad. Weddings usually made women feel very romantic. That could work to his advantage.

'Martini,' Amanda croaked. 'A big one.'

Harrison spared a glance for her friend.

'Double olives in mine.' Nicole grinned.

The redhead was cute, he thought, but he had eyes only for Amanda. Why hadn't his mother told him how beautiful she was?

He beckoned to the bartender and placed the order, though he felt as if he'd already had about a dozen of the potent cocktails.

Why would Amanda Whitfield need an arranged date? The mystery of it captured his interest as completely as her face captured his imagination. Good thing his imagination was big enough to entertain thoughts of her long, curling blonde hair. He had no problem imagining *that* spread across his pillow. It would be easy to forget his purpose in being here tonight.

If his mother hadn't set this up . . . If he hadn't seen her treat that guy so rudely just because he was trying to talk to her . . .

'I must say, Amanda, you aren't anything like what I imagined.'

'You're nothing like what I had hoped either.' She blushed bright red. 'Imagined. I meant imagined.'

Her slip of the tongue shocked Harrison back to reality. Cringing, he remembered what he looked like. He felt his own face flush. To her eyes, he must look like a refugee from the war between the sexes. Discomfited, he could hardly manage to pay for the drinks when they arrived.

What had possessed him to wet down his hair and wear such an outlandish suit? If only he'd worn his usual clothes — what his mom called the *GQ* look.

The polyester suit he'd found at a charity resale shop was hideous in the extreme. He'd outwitted himself this time. Looking like this, Harrison knew he didn't stand a chance with a woman like Amanda.

The only thing he'd get from tonight's date was the accomplishment of his first goal. She'd reject him outright as an escort to her relative's wedding. Of course, that was what he had wanted — before he'd seen her.

'I'm beginning to feel invisible,' Nicole muttered.

Harrison chuckled ruefully. He'd blown it, but good. 'Forgive me, Nicole.

Let me be the first to say you're very visible — and a pleasant visibility it is.'

Nicole nodded appreciatively. 'That's more like it. I truly believe that flattery will get anyone anywhere.'

Harrison looked at Amanda. 'Do you believe in that too?'

'Not really. I prefer the truth — if not in word, then in deed. It may be a cliché, but I really do think actions speak louder than words. So, I prefer to look beneath the surface for truth.'

What a crock! Harrison suppressed the words that rang out in his mind. Like hell she did! She couldn't see the real man at all. He stared at her, willing her to look beneath his surface.

Amanda looked away from his probing dark eyes, which appeared three times bigger than normal due to his thick lenses.

To her dismay, something about him made her pulse accelerate. That scent reached her again, tantalizing in its complexity. Surely she wasn't attracted to him? The very thought horrified her.

She had to get rid of him before she did something foolish — like accept him as her escort to the wedding!

'Would you excuse us, please?' Amanda picked up her handbag and slid off the high bar stool.

'Sure.' Harrison stood. Intently, his eyes searched her sapphire blue ones. Did she feel that sense of connection too? Regretfully, he decided that she probably didn't. She was obviously blinded by his appearance.

'Nicole?' Amanda looked at her friend and was surprised to see her staring raptly at Harrison. 'Come on, Nicole.'

'Huh?' Nicole turned to Amanda.

'Ladies' room.'

'Oh! Sorry I was lost in thought. Back in a jiffy, Harrison.'

In the ladies' room, Amanda snapped open her red suede clutch bag. 'You aren't helping by flirting with him,' she charged.

'What do you mean? I wasn't flirting.'

'Then what do you call it?' Amanda

dug through her purse for her lipstick.

'Being nice! Geez, what are you so upset about?'

Uncapping her lipstick, Amanda said, 'I'm upset because he's worse than I imagined. I'll never, ever accept another blind date as long as I live.'

'Aw, come on. He's not that bad.'

'Not that bad?' Amanda threw her hands up. 'Look. Just tell me how to get rid of him.'

'Are you sure you want to?' Nicole asked. She crossed her arms and faced Amanda.

'Nicole!' Amanda stared, aghast, at her friend. 'Don't be ridiculous. I can't be seen with him in public!'

'I am completely serious. Think a minute. He's got the greatest voice! It's husky and sexy. If you close your eyes, he sounds seductive as all get out!'

'Oh, great. Maybe I could wear a blindfold to the wedding.'

'And he's tall and seems to be well-built. I think there's more muscles under that polyester than you'd think.'

'Yeah, but what about that polyester?'

'Hear me out. He looks to be nicely tanned — at least his hands and face are.'

'Yeah, maybe he put suntan oil on his hair. That would explain that wet look.'

'You know, with the right clothes and with his hair fixed, he might clean up real good.'

'You must be kidding!' Without retouching her lipstick, Amanda capped the gold tube and tossed it into her purse.

'No, I'm not. Amanda, I think he just might do.' Excitement colored her voice.

'How many martinis have you had?' Amanda demanded.

'Probably not enough. Think about it. Look at him and imagine an Armani suit. Ignore that greased-down hair and think freshly washed and styled — thick, silky black hair. Just removing those glasses would improve his face a hundred percent.'

'Those glasses give him fish eyes.'

Amanda shuddered. 'I don't know. It's hard to believe anyone who looks so weird could become an acceptable escort.'

'Close your eyes and remember his voice.'

'And his smell,' Amanda said suddenly.

'His what?' Nicole asked, her gaze swinging from the mirror to Amanda's face.

'He has this — this odor.' Amanda blushed. 'I mean it doesn't stink. It's . . . tantalizing.' She wouldn't admit under threat of torture that it made heat pool in certain unmentionable parts of her body.

'Tantalizing?' Nicole frowned.

'Well, yes. It must be some new aftershave. I need to find out what it is. Purely for research purposes, of course,' she hurried to add.

'Forget business for now. First things first. You need to persuade him to go to the wedding with you. Then we've got to figure out a way to make him over.'

'By Valentine's Day?'

'Sure! I think he has real potential.'

'You're dreaming. This is hopeless.' Amanda felt like wringing her hands in despair.

'No. No, it isn't. Don't give up so easy. Remember that vow you made when you got the invitation? To find a guy to take you to the wedding?'

'Yeah, but I said I would find a gorgeous, smart, successful date. Harrison Kincaid isn't any of those — except maybe smart and successful — and you can't tell that by looking at him.'

'Ah-ha! So looks *are* of primary importance to you, despite what you said.'

'Quit giving me a hard time.'

'Come on, Amanda. Where's your spirit of adventure?'

'I used it all up coming here tonight.'

'I really think he might work out. Besides, it's not like you have a lot of options. He seems to be your last resort. After all, there's no denying you are at that awkward age.'

'Yeah, twenty-eight and never been compromised,' Amanda replied sourly.

'That wasn't quite what I meant.' Nicole shrugged. 'I'll say it again. You could decide not to go to the lousy wedding.'

'That's not an option. My mother would have a cow if I missed it. Unfortunately, Marcy is family.' She blinked away sudden tears. 'I just wanted to show her for once. You wouldn't believe the note she sent with her invitation.'

'What did it say?'

'That I could bring a date — if I could get one.'

'What! Why, that — '

'Don't say it.' Amanda's mouth set in a stubborn line. 'I didn't go to my senior prom, Nicole. I never went to the formals in college, but Marcy went to everything. She always had a date. And she always knew I didn't. Now she's getting married, and I still don't even have a boyfriend. I'm beginning to think Mr. Right is in the same category as the tooth fairy and the Easter bunny.'

'Forget Mr. Right. You haven't even found Mr. Maybe,' Nicole muttered. At the wounded look that crossed Amanda's face, she added, 'Sorry. I didn't mean that. You have lots of male friends. Surely one of them could take you to the wedding?'

'I've already asked. They're all busy on Valentine's Day with their girlfriends. Do you know how hard it is to find a date for the most romantic day of the year — and to a wedding of all things? Men act as if they'll come down with a severe case of matrimony if they get within a few feet of an actual wedding ceremony.'

Amanda sighed heavily. Her eyes met Nicole's in the mirror. 'You're absolutely right. Harrison Kincaid is my last resort.'

'I'm so sorry, Amanda,' Nicole said sympathetically.

'I'm not giving Marcy a chance to comment again about my failings as a woman. Any man is better than no man.' She shuddered. 'I don't care what Harrison looks like.' She took a deep breath. 'He's not getting away.'

'All right, Amanda! That's the spirit. Let's do it!'

Amanda nodded her head emphatically and took a deep breath. 'Now, how do you propose to get him to agree to a makeover? Even with my limited experience, I'm fairly certain men aren't into that sort of thing.'

'Hmm.' Nicole pursed her lips and eyed her friend thoughtfully. 'Well, you'll have to sweet talk him. Use your charm. That's what you said you were going to do.'

'Is that the best advice you can offer?' Amanda stared, aghast.

Nicole shrugged. 'If that fails, maybe you could kiss him. It's supposed to work for frogs.'

5

Harrison decided he couldn't blame Amanda and her friend for treating him as if he were an ugly cow dog. After all, nobody had forced him to alter his appearance the way he had.

While he waited for Amanda and her friend to return, he faced the fact that he'd blown it. No matter how hard he tried, he couldn't think of a way to undo the damage.

Somehow, he couldn't imagine Amanda, or any woman, would be thrilled if he said, 'Oh, by the way, I really look a lot better than this. I just couldn't stand the thought of another blind date with one of my mother's less than appealing finds.'

Yeah. That bit of honesty would be as welcome as a tornado in the spring. Harrison sighed. He might as well cut his losses and leave. Staying any longer than necessary with Amanda would only make him regret the situation more. There was something about her that appealed to him enormously. It wasn't just looks. He always had access to great-looking women. With a sigh, he decided philosophically that he and Amanda were just two ships passing in the night.

He stood when he saw them approaching. After helping them with their chairs, he sat down and gathered his thoughts. He didn't want to tell Amanda good-bye, but it had to be done.

Before he could speak, Amanda asked in a bright, perky voice that sounded as false as his appearance.

'Why don't you tell me about your work, Harrison?'

'My work?' he asked, puzzled by her sudden interest.

'Yes. I'm sure it's absolutely fascinating.' She smiled at him and leaned closer.

For a moment, he thought she was

going to bat those long black eyelashes at him.

'I'm sure it would just bore you. Computer technology isn't something that seems to attract beautiful blondes.'

Her smile disappeared and her brows snapped together. 'Why? Do you think I wouldn't understand it? Maybe you think blondes are too dumb to comprehend complex issues?'

'No. Of course not.' Her response fascinated him as much as it amused him. 'I was trying to be gallant and flattering,' he added. 'I must need some practice.'

'Oh,' Amanda said. 'Sorry, I guess I'm kind of sensitive about some things.'

He'd certainly uncovered one of her hot buttons, he thought, bringing his palm up to cover his mouth in what he hoped she perceived as a thoughtful pose. He sure didn't want her to see him grinning. Maybe she'd heard one blonde joke too many.

'I might know more about the subject

of computers than you realize,' she continued.

'No, you don't,' Nicole gibed. 'I have to explain to you every time you get near a computer about how to open, save, and close files.'

'Just because I don't know specifics doesn't mean I can't grasp theory.'

What a bundle of contradictions she was. Harrison looked at her and smiled. Make that a delightful bundle of contradictions.

'I'll be glad to explain my work to you, Amanda.' He sipped his drink. 'Let's see. What do you know about computer language?'

Amanda looked smug. 'You mean DOS.'

'No. Not really. I mean FORTRAN, COBOL, or BASIC.'

'Oh.' Amanda swirled her untouched martini. 'Well, not too much,' she reluctantly admitted.

'Exactly. Neither did most people our age. That's why the Y2K bug became such a huge problem. Most of the computers used by business and government, worldwide, were programmed years ago using computer languages that are basically obsolete now. For example, programmers used COBOL, or Common Business Oriented Language, to write computer programs for banks.'

'I've heard of FORTRAN,' Nicole crowed. 'That was what industry used, wasn't it?'

Harrison nodded. 'Right. There're a lot of other computer languages too, and they were all specialized for different applications.'

'So what does that have to do with you?' Amanda asked, genuine curiosity in her voice.

'Well, the programmers who wrote those programs and worked on those projects had long since retired by the time everyone realized that the turning of the century would create a problem for any computer that couldn't recognize a four-digit date. Any computer programmed for two-digit dates would read the year after ninety-nine as zero-zero, or 1900.'

Amanda and Nicole both nodded. 'Sure, everyone knows that,' Amanda said. 'I could never understand why it wasn't a simple matter to just tell the computer it was the year two thousand.'

'Because you had to speak its language to tell it. Most programming is done in C ++ nowadays.'

'Ah,' Amanda said, 'you had to speak FORTRAN or whatever.'

'Exactly. If your computer speaks COBOL, it won't understand if you try to give it instructions in C ++. So, I put together a company and lured those early programmers out of retirement. I learned from them, and together we contracted with government — domestic and foreign — to solve the problems inherent in the systems.'

'Wow! So you kind of saved the planet — just like Superman or Bruce Willis,' Nicole said.

Harrison shrugged. 'I don't know about saving the planet, but we've had our hands full the last couple of years.'

He glanced at Amanda to see her reaction. He was afraid that the conversation had bored her.

'You really are a genius,' Amanda said. 'Just like your mother told us.'

Harrison wanted to groan. He'd wanted to impress her, he admitted. Instead, it seemed that he'd just confirmed in her mind the fact that he really was a cyber geek.

'So what are you doing now? We've obviously made it past the millennium mark and civilization as we know it didn't crumble. Are there any other threats to the computer world lurking around the corner?' Amanda asked.

'Nothing major that I know of. We're doing a little of this and a little of that. For the present, we're investing a lot of time in a virtual reality project.'

'Oh, cool!' Nicole said. 'When you work with something like that, I can't imagine you sit around and play computer games for fun. So what do you do when you want to play?'

'Do for fun?' Harrison asked, wrinkling his brow. He looked at Amanda. She seemed to be trying to fade into the woodwork. Ah! Understanding dawned. Nicole was trying, albeit not too subtly, to lead up to the matter of the wedding.

'You know — fun,' Amanda echoed with a weak smile.

Nicole chimed in. 'Like fine dining, live entertainment — '

'As opposed to dead entertainment?' Harrison asked dryly.

Nicole grinned and continued, 'Dancing, fabulous desserts. High society highjinks.'

He quirked a dark brow. 'High society highjinks? And just what would that be?' He was having difficulty believing that Amanda wanted him to escort her to that wedding.

'Nicole's mouth runneth over,' Amanda muttered. 'What she's trying to describe is — '

'A wedding,' Harrison finished her sentence.

'Your mother guaranteed you'd take

Amanda to her cousin's wedding,' Nicole baldly declared.

'She guaranteed?' Harrison waited for Amanda to say his service as an escort wasn't necessary, but she remained silent, allowing her friend to engage in the arm-twisting.

Harrison was fascinated. Could Amanda have another motive in wanting to go with him? Was she interested in him or his money, he suddenly wondered. Maybe she had found out how much he was worth. It wasn't a secret, but not too many people knew he was one of Houston's newest multimillionaires.

He looked Amanda over — expensive dress, red suede shoes and purse that probably cost as much or more than the dress. Was it possible that she was looking for someone to support her in the style to which she was obviously accustomed? Try as he could, he couldn't find any other reason for her wanting to date him. He'd seen how he looked in the mirror — not even close to a young woman's dream. So what was the game here? This just added another dimension to his already considerable curiosity about Amanda Whitfield.

He decided to see how serious she was about dating him. He frowned — convincingly, he hoped. 'Well, I told my mother I'd meet you, but I don't know about going with you to this wedding. That seems like such an intimate occasion.'

'Oh, it's not, believe me,' Amanda said.

'Yeah, not intimate at all. Why, there will be six hundred fifty invited guests. You'll just be a face in the crowd.'

He frowned some more. 'I don't know if I'd feel comfortable in that kind of situation. I mean, we hardly know each other.'

'No problem. There's plenty of time for you and Amanda to have several dates between now and the wedding,' Nicole declared.

'That's well and good for you to say,

Nicole.' Harrison studied Amanda. Just how badly did she want him? She didn't seem nearly as eager as her friend to see him again. 'What does Amanda say?'

Amanda had remained silent, trying to figure a way out of the sticky situation. Was Nicole right? Could they make Harrison into a proper escort in a couple of weeks? She sighed. She didn't have any other options.

Feeling resigned, she asked, 'Do you know how to dance, Harrison?'

He shook his head. 'Afraid not,' he lied.

Darn. Her first impression was right, Amanda thought. The guy had nothing going for him except a sexy voice and an irresistible smell.

'No problem,' Nicole said cheerfully. 'We can teach you.'

Amanda shot a withering glance in her direction. This was ridiculous. She'd just call the whole thing off. Amanda took a deep breath — and got a lungful of that intoxicating scent again.

Delicately, she sniffed. What was it? She could easily recognize all the popular men's aftershave lotions and colognes. This was nothing like any of them.

Amanda exhaled quickly, leaned toward him, and inhaled again, relishing the way her perception of the scent traveled through the neural pathways and wrapped around her nerve endings. Her eyes closed so her sense of smell would be heightened.

'Is there a problem, Amanda?' Harrison asked.

'What do you mean?' she asked, lost in sensation.

'You seem to — ' He broke off. He grinned and shook his head. 'How shall I put this? If you were a cocker spaniel, I'd think you were trying to make my acquaintance.'

Amanda blushed at his perception. He *was* sharp. She'd already decided, after hearing about the company he'd started, that he might actually be the genius his mother asserted he was.

'I'm sorry. I'm a perfumer, so I'm always intrigued by scents. The one you're wearing is different from anything I've smelled before. What is it?'

Nicole spread her hands in a gesture of exasperation. 'I just don't smell anything.'

'I'm not wearing any cologne.' Harrison looked bewildered. He frowned. 'What exactly is a perfumer?'

'I design fragrances. Nicole and I own a boutique called Scent From Heaven.' Amanda discreetly sniffed again.

'You must be wearing some new fragrance,' she insisted. He might have lousy taste in clothes — and hair styles — but his smell was indescribable — so alluring it made her want to snuggle closer to him. She had to know what it was. Then it would lose its ability to mesmerize her. Heavens! If she could bottle that, she could make a fortune.

'I promise you. I'm not wearing anything,' Harrison insisted.

Not wearing anything?

For some reason those words triggered her imagination and created a startling picture in her brain. What on earth was wrong with her? Maybe her biological clock was ticking so loudly that it was making her insane.

Was she so desperate that she'd stooped to fantasizing about geeks? But when she closed her eyes, which she proceeded to do, and smelled him — and listened to him speak — she forgot his nerdy appearance.

His voice was the kind of voice a woman wanted in a man — strong without being harsh. It was the kind of voice a woman could easily imagine whispering words of love in a darkened room.

'Am I keeping you past your bedtime?' that sexy voice asked.

Amanda's eyes flew open. 'Of course not.' She knew she must look like an idiot. 'I was just . . . ' she trailed off. She couldn't tell him she was fantasizing about him.

'She was just meditating,' Nicole

tossed in. 'She does that every night at this time.'

Harrison's lips twitched. Amazing as it seemed, Amanda Whitfield actually wanted him as her date. Maybe if he hung around her some, he'd figure out why. If nothing else, he wouldn't be bored. He couldn't recall when he'd had such fun. Certainly not with the last woman he'd dated.

'Meditating? Do you chant a mantra or something?' In fact, that was one reason he'd broken up with the woman lawyer he'd been seeing. She had no sense of humor. Plenty of arrogance, but no humor.

'No, she just closes her eyes and breathes — ouch!' Nicole yelped.

Harrison pretended he hadn't seen Amanda pinch her friend. In his opinion, a sense of humor was as important as good sex in a relationship. Though he hadn't dated the same woman more than once since he'd broken it off with the self-absorbed lawyer — who hadn't possessed either of those qualities — he just couldn't say no to a second date with Amanda. And maybe a third date too. Who knows? He'd just see where this led. Maybe he was ready for a little steady relationship.

'I guess we better make sure we don't have our first dance lesson at this time. I wouldn't want to foul up your meditation schedule,' he said.

When he reached inside his coat, Amanda cringed when she saw the white plastic pocket protector. He pulled out a card and handed it to her.

Harrison leaned forward, inundating her with his scent. 'Call me when you want to give me that dance lesson.'

Mesmerized by her body's reaction to him, she could only nod as he stood.

She watched him saunter toward the door — and saunter was the perfect word to describe his sexy, rolling gait.

'How can he walk like that and talk like that?' Nicole asked.

'And smell like that?' Amanda added.

'And be such a geek?' they asked each other in unison.

6

'I know I said any man would do, but there are limits.' Amanda sighed, turning to look askance at her best friend. 'Aren't there?'

'Don't think of him as a geek. Think of him as stylistically challenged.' At Amanda's sour expression, Nicole added, 'Don't like that, huh? Then how about technologically advantaged?'

Amanda's expression brooked no nonsense. 'No, I prefer to think of him as the guy who's doing me a favor. That keeps it in the proper perspective.'

'You have to admit he is a nice guy. He could have been a real dork. But he's smart and has a good sense of humor.'

'Maybe that will be enough to appease my mother.'

'She'll be deliriously happy.'

'Until she sees him. Then she'll be

just plain delirious,' Amanda muttered.

'Not to worry. We'll have him transformed into Prince Charming by the time she meets him.'

Amanda looked at her watch, then slid off the bar stool. 'I'll see you tomorrow.'

'Where are you going?'

'I think I'll stop by and tell Mom now. Then maybe I'll go kiss a few frogs. I'm going to need all the practice I can get.'

'Cool,' Nicole said. She watched her friend walk away, drawing the eyes of every man in the place. As usual, Amanda was oblivious to the attention she attracted.

Nicole grinned and gave in to the laughter that had threatened to erupt all evening. If Amanda had any real experience with men, she'd have known that Harrison Kincaid's charisma and his looks just didn't compute.

No man who walked like that and talked like that could be a geek. What was his game? She didn't know, but she did know one thing: Harrison Kincaid had the hots for Amanda.

Nicole had a feeling that Amanda had got a lot more than she had bargained for with this blind date. She giggled. The Fourth of July might be months away, but she had a feeling that Amanda and Harrison were about to create a fireworks spectacle. Leaning back, she sipped her martini and let the cool piano music wash over her.

★　★　★

Amanda chatted with Darla a few minutes, then headed to her car. Wind grabbed her hair and tangled it about her face. The blue norther still had Houston in its grip.

The drive from the club on the Richmond strip to her parents' home near the Galleria took only a half hour. Amanda rehearsed what she was going to say until she pulled into their driveway. A moment of panic assailed her, but she convinced herself that

Harrison would look immeasurably better by the day of the wedding. If he didn't, she'd personally strangle Nicole for talking her into this.

Amanda used her house key to let herself in. The buttery aroma of popcorn hit her immediately. Gunfire and screams came from the den. She grinned. Obviously, her dad was watching his favorite kind of movies — action adventure with a high body count.

'Mom? Dad?' she called, walking toward the noise.

'In here, baby,' her father called out.

Smiling, Amanda kicked off her shoes when she reached the den. 'Umm, popcorn.' She settled next to her father, and kissed him on the cheek. English Leather. She laid her head on his shoulder, feeling comforted by the smell that he'd worn since she'd been a child.

Even though Leland Whitfield could afford expensive designer colognes, he clung to the aftershave of his youth. Amanda hoped he never changed.

That's why she'd never created a perfume for him or for her mother who still used White Shoulders.

'Where's Mom?' She helped herself to a handful of corn.

'She's in the shower. She just finished her torture session on the treadmill.'

'How's the diet and exercise program?'

Leland rolled his eyes. 'Don't ask. Just eat faster. This has to be out of sight by the time she gets in here.'

'That bad, huh?'

'Why do I have to diet every time she wants to lose ten pounds? She doesn't even need to lose ten pounds. She looks perfectly fine.'

'I agree. It's Aunt Gwen. You know how she and Mom are.'

'I wish the two of them had left sibling rivalry back in childhood where it belongs. Sure would make my life a lot simpler.'

'Anything good on TV?' Amanda grabbed another handful of corn.

'It's one of those Dolph Lundgren

movies,' Leland said through a mouthful of popcorn.

From the master bedroom, a voice called out, 'Is that popcorn I smell?'

'Quick! Hide this!' Leland said, thrusting the bowl at Amanda.

Giggling, she ran to the kitchen and opened the oven door and shoved the bowl into the cold oven. Then she hurried back and plopped on the couch next to her dad, who was wiping his salty fingers on the sides of his jeans.

'Oh, is this the movie that was filmed in Houston?' Amanda asked, winking at her father. 'It's in the oven,' she mouthed.

He nodded. 'Yeah,' Leland said, a little too loud. 'This is the one where the alien pumps cocaine into his victims, then sucks the endorphins out of their brains.'

'Yuk!' Susie Whitfield said, coming up and leaning over the sofa. 'Where's Cary Grant when you need him?'

'Dead — probably from dieting,' Leland replied.

'Just ignore your father. He hasn't had any red meat in a week so he's a little grouchy.' Susie kissed Amanda on the cheek, leaving a delightful whiff of her perfume in the air. 'What a nice surprise!'

'I just thought I'd drop by and tell you the big news,' Amanda said with fake heartiness.

'You're engaged!' Susie clapped her hands together. 'Oh, Leland, Amanda finally found a man!'

'No, Mom, I'm not engaged,' Amanda said with long-suffering impatience.

'Oh, then what's the news?'

'I have a date for Marcy's wedding.'

'Oh, dear. I'd mentioned to Buddy Marlowe that you might have need of his services as an escort again. He's such a nice man, dear, even if he is a little older than your generation.'

'Mom, he's nearly as old as Daddy!'

'He's a good ten years younger than your father. And he is handsome. And single. And rich.'

'And he has hands like an octopus!'

'What?' Susie roared. 'Do you mean that two-faced, devious son of — ' She clamped his lips together. 'Sorry, baby.'

Amanda grinned. 'That's okay, Mom. I heard worse than that in high school.'

'Just wait till I give him a piece of my mind,' Leland fumed.

'Daddy, I'm a big girl. I can handle situations like that. You're sweet, but I don't need you to protect my honor.'

Harrison Kincaid didn't seem so bad when compared to the other men she'd gone out with, Amanda thought.

'Let's not talk about the unpleasant Mr. Marlowe,' Susie said. 'I should have known there was something wrong with a guy who was still single at his age. The old goat!'

Her mother's changed attitude amused Amanda. When her mother asked about her date for the wedding, Amanda willingly changed the subject and began the little speech she'd rehearsed.

'Well, my date is Harrison Kincaid. He's very smart — brilliant, in fact

— and he owns a computer company.'

'What's his name?' Leland asked, punching the mute button on the television.

When Amanda repeated it, Leland frowned. 'I've heard that name before. I think I saw an article about him in that magazine about Texas entrepreneurs,' Leland said. He looked at the neatly stacked magazines on the shelf below the coffee table. 'It's around here someplace.'

Susie's brow knit in thought. 'I know that name, too. Give me a minute, and it'll come to me.'

Amanda raced ahead and told them all about his company and his virtual reality project, emphasizing all the positive aspects she could think of.

Susie quit frowning and laughed delightedly. 'So he's rich and single and brilliant. Just wait till I tell Gwen about this! I'm so sick of her bragging about Marcy's lawyer fiancé as if it's something remarkable that a lawyer is marrying another lawyer. How boring!'

'Why don't you and Gwen grow up?' Leland exclaimed.

'Never mind your father, dear. Tell me, what does your young man look like?'

'Oh, well, uh, he's got a fantastic smile and a really great personality,' Amanda said.

'A great personality?' Her mother's voice was ominous.

Amanda just couldn't tell her mother the truth, but maybe she should prepare her in case the makeover didn't succeed.

'Yes, Mom. He's not one of those men who are overly concerned with fashion and, uh, looks.'

'He's not?' Susie frowned. 'Oh, dear.'

'Good for him,' Leland said. 'He sounds like he might be a real man.'

Amanda laughed. 'Daddy, anyone who didn't know you would think you were a cow puncher or a roughneck instead of an executive with an insurance company.'

'Hey! Executives can be macho.' He

grinned. 'All kidding aside, too many guys today are more concerned with the way their hair looks than with their careers or their character.'

'Why don't you bring him over for dinner?' Susie suggested. 'We could get acquainted before the wedding.'

'I don't know. I just met him. It's not as if we're having a hot romance.'

'Oh.' Her mother's mouth turned down at the corners.

'Sorry to disappoint you, Mom. I'll check with him, but he may be too busy. I'll let you know.'

Feeling she'd done the best she could for the moment, Amanda changed the subject. She told them about all the special orders she'd received for Valentine's Day.

'You really look tired, baby,' her dad said a short while later. 'Want to spend the night in your old room?'

'Thanks, Daddy, but I'll go on home. You're right. I really am exhausted.' Tomorrow was going to be a long day. She planned to call Harrison as soon as she got to her boutique in the morning.

Somehow, she'd find the energy to get her work done tomorrow and conduct a dance lesson tomorrow night. The sooner the better. She had the feeling that Harrison would need all the lessons she could give him.

Her heart fluttered at the thought of dancing with him. She couldn't explain the vision that popped into her head — she and Harrison snuggled up close while they swayed, cheek to cheek, to a sultry torch song. It made no sense when it was even money that the guy probably had two left feet.

*   *   *

On the way home, Harrison picked up his cell phone and called his buddy Jim.

'Nguyen, you still at the office?'

'Obviously since that's where you've called. I was working on the VR project. What do you want? I was on my way out.'

'Just thought I'd cancel our plans to

go to the Rockets game tomorrow night.' Excitement bubbled inside him. He knew Amanda would call soon — he felt it in his bones — and he planned to be ready.

'You get a better offer?' Jim laughed.

'Something like that.'

Harrison would certainly call Amanda Whitfield a much better offer. 'I'm going to take dance lessons.'

'Dance lessons?'

'Right.'

'Excuse me for mentioning this, Harrison, but we were in the same dance class in college. Remember? You talked me into taking ballroom dancing for one of our Phys Ed credits because it was a great way to meet girls?'

'Yeah, and we met some fantastic ones, didn't we?'

'True, but I barely pulled a C in the class. You, on the other hand, aced it,' he grumbled.

'Don't whine, Jim, it's not a macho thing to do.'

'I should have blackmailed you big

time. If I'd told the instructor that you'd won some kind of trophy for dancing — '

'Water under the bridge, my friend,' Harrison interrupted with a laugh. 'I'm not going to feel sorry for you, so just shut up and listen.' They made plans to go to the game another night.

'This girl must be a doozy,' Jim said. 'Stay out of trouble, Kincaid.'

'Can't guarantee that,' Harrison laughed. 'Can't guarantee that at all.'

Somehow, he had a feeling that the beautiful Amanda Whitfield was nothing but trouble. But she was the kind of trouble that made life interesting.

'Just don't forget that flavor of the week beats plain vanilla every day. You taught me that too.'

Jim switched topics and began discussing a defective microchip he'd found in the game prototype they were building. Harrison listened with half an ear.

The evening had been nothing like what he'd expected. He could hardly wait to see Amanda again. He grinned. Would Nicole be along next time to chaperone them and expedite their dating? An inspiration hit.

'Hey, Jim,' he interrupted.

'Yeah?'

'Are you still seeing that chiropractor?'

'Nah! She broke it off. Said I was only going out with her to get free adjustments.'

'Were you?'

'Not at first. You know how it is. She did have the greatest hands, though,' Jim admitted with a laugh.

'How do you like redheads?'

'Don't know. Never dated one.'

'That's about to change, good buddy. If you're willing?'

'Sounds interesting. We'll talk about it tomorrow. Right now I've got to go. Got a dinner date with a dentist.'

Harrison didn't know what was funnier — Amanda's dread of seeing him again or Nicole's unexpected enthusiasm.

Somehow, he didn't think he'd have to wait long to get a phone call for a dancing date. But who would it come from? Amanda the reluctant or Nicole the instigator?

Harrison had always believed that divide-and-conquer was an effective strategy. With a little help from Jim, he figured he'd be able to separate Amanda from her partner in crime.

Then he'd discover what made Amanda Whitfield tick. For a moment, he regretted that he'd uncover her secrets. Take away the mystery, and she might turn out to be like all the other women he'd dated — lovely, predictable, and easily forgettable.

7

'The lab isn't exactly the kind of setting I'd pick for a romantic dance lesson,' Nicole teased. She helped herself to a handful of the candy hearts from the crystal dish on Amanda's desk.

'This is not about romance.' Amanda tucked her hands into the pockets of her white lab coat. 'The lab is perfect because it has so much open floor space. Besides, the last thing I want is for Harrison to get the wrong idea.'

Nicole looked her over and winced. 'Is that the reason for the spinster's bun, that rag of a dress, and those old lady shoes?'

'Of course.' Amanda held her right foot up. The black leather lace-up shoes had no redeeming features. 'You'd think shoes this ugly would be more comfortable.'

Nicole giggled. 'My great-grandmother

used to wear shoes just like that. They looked better on her than on you.'

'Thanks a lot.' Amanda walked over to the long counter where she did most of her work and began cleaning up from a long day of experimenting with different evergreen scents.

'You know you can't have it both ways.' Nicole climbed up on one of the high stools next to the counter and watched as Amanda pulled on a pair of rubber gloves and plunged her hands into a sink full of soapy water.

'What do you mean?' Amanda paused in washing a glass beaker and turned to look at Nicole.

'A few days ago you were bemoaning the fact that men never asked you for a date because they were intimidated by your beauty.'

'No, *you* said they were intimidated,' Amanda corrected. 'I personally think I just don't have sex appeal.'

Nicole waved her hands as if to dismiss Amanda's protest. 'Now you're saying that Harrison will succumb to you if you don't look like Grandma Moses.'

Amanda frowned and rinsed the beaker, then put it in a drain rack. 'Well, he's not exactly a normal man. He might feel so encouraged because I'm going out with him that he would read more into it than he should.'

Nicole whooped with laughter. 'If anyone else said that, I'd think she was stuck on herself. Fortunately, I know that's not the case with you.'

'You're the one who was so concerned that I might use and abuse him. I'd hate for him to think that there was more to this than escorting me to the wedding.'

'Amanda Whitfield! You big snob!' Nicole chided.

Amanda pursed her lips. 'I'm not a snob.' She jerked off the rubber gloves and laid them over the sink edge.

'Yes, you are. You were moaning and groaning because no one ever asks you out, and you said you'd be glad if anyone — I repeat — anyone, asked you for a date.'

Amanda shifted uncomfortably. 'Well, I didn't expect someone like him.'

'You're just as guilty as everyone else — judging a person by his looks. That's what men do when they see you, and that's what you're doing to Harrison.'

'Goodness, I didn't know you and he were such good friends.' Nicole's words made Amanda uncomfortable. 'Are you saying that beneath that unattractive exterior beats the heart of a Don Juan?'

'Well, I wouldn't go that far. Maybe the heart of a nice guy?'

'Exactly! He does seem like a nice guy. I don't want to hurt his feelings by making him think there's more to this than a date of convenience.'

'If I remember correctly, he wasn't exactly falling at your feet in adoration.'

'Thanks for reminding me. That's really an ego boost.'

'Hey, judging by your previous statement, your ego doesn't need any boosting.' Nicole's grin took the sting from her words.

Amanda dried her hands on a paper

towel. 'You're probably right.' She held up both hands in a gesture of surrender. 'I guess I'm over-reacting.'

'I know what your problem is. You feel a little guilty because you are using him.'

Amanda sighed. 'Okay. You're right. I am using him, and I feel bad about it. There, I said it. Are you happy now?'

'Relax. I have a feeling Harrison Kincaid, despite his appearance, doesn't let himself be used unless he wants to be.'

'I hope you're right. It would make me feel a lot better if I thought he was in this just to have a few laughs and a good time.'

Nicole grinned. 'Then you can definitely relax. I believe that's precisely what he's looking for — a good time.' She slid off the stool. 'Or maybe the only reason he's doing this is because his mother is making him.'

'That's not a very flattering thing to say about a grown man.'

'Maybe not, but be thankful that he minds his mommy.'

'You're terrible.' Amanda smiled grudgingly.

'You're really going to think I'm terrible when I tell you that I can only stay for an hour tonight.'

'What?' Panic shot through Amanda. 'But . . . but,' she sputtered. 'You can't leave me alone with him.'

'Why not? Anyway, I've got to stop by my mother's, or she's threatened to report me as a missing person.'

The security buzzer prevented further discussion.

'He's here!' Amanda patted her hair. 'How do I look?'

'Hideous!' Nicole grinned.

'Good. Good.' She started to leave the room to answer the door, then stopped and turned to Nicole. 'Do you honestly think we can whip him into shape in time for the wedding? I've tried, but I can't come up with a polite way to suggest to him that he let us pick out his clothes. And how do you tell

93

him he's not just having a bad hair day? He's having a bad hair decade?'

★   ★   ★

Harrison's mouth twitched. Amanda looked as if she'd taken as much pains with her appearance as he had with his. The drab, shapeless gray dress beneath her white lab coat successfully hid the body that the red dress had displayed so spectacularly the night he'd met her.

He'd had a tough time finding another suit as ugly as the brown and orange plaid, but he'd given it the old college try and finally had found one in the dollar-an-item barrel at the same thrift store.

This suit — a navy blue with a blindingly yellow shirt — wasn't as obnoxiously patterned as his first one, but what it lacked in pattern, it made up for in style. The lapels were so wide you could have parked a Metro bus on them, and the trouser legs belled out more than a sailor's pants.

Harrison actually found himself admiring the old-fashioned polyester fabric. What else could be washed and dried and come out without a wrinkle and with trouser creases sharp enough to slice bread? He choked back the urge to laugh when Amanda stared at him, her mouth opening and closing as if at a loss for words.

Somehow he didn't think she was admiring the miracle fabric or his slicked-down hair. Of course, that bun she'd twisted her blond curls into wouldn't take any hair styling awards.

Amanda couldn't believe her eyes. Where did Harrison buy his clothes? And how was she going to persuade him to let her take him shopping for a wedding suit?

'Come in,' she murmured, trying not to look into his magnified eyes through the glass lenses. 'You're right on time.'

'I asked one of my friends to join us.' Harrison glanced behind him. 'He should be here any minute.'

'A friend?' Amanda asked, puzzled. 'But why?'

'He wants to learn to dance too.' Once again, he looked over his shoulder. He grinned. 'Here he comes now.'

Amanda was almost afraid to look. If Harrison's friend had the same taste in clothes — twenty-year-old thrift shop chic — she knew she'd break down and cackle out loud.

To her relief, Harrison's friend was an extremely attractive Asian dressed in a pair of beautiful brown wool slacks, a creamy white starched dress shirt, and a tan cable knit cardigan adorned with leather-wrapped buttons. He wore Polo which suited him well, but it didn't have the same alluring odor as Harrison's cologne, she noted. Harrison's brand, though faint, was something she could recognize in a dark room.

'New suit, Harrison?' Jim asked, looking him over.

Harrison grinned. 'Yeah, you like it?'

'Uh, I think it's a memorable

addition to your wardrobe.'

After he made the introductions, and they had exchanged pleasantries, Amanda locked the boutique's door and led them through the showroom to the back.

'Harrison brought his friend Jim Nguyen,' Amanda said by way of introduction to Nicole. 'Jim, my best friend and my partner Nicole Patrick.'

Amanda recognized the flare of interest in Nicole's eyes. She had to admit that Jim was something to look at. Definitely more dazzling than Harrison. 'Jim wants to learn to dance also.'

Jim walked over to Nicole and lifted her hand to his lips in a courtly gesture that should have looked ridiculous but didn't.

'Actually, I know the basics. I just need to brush up a little.'

'I'm your girl then. Let's brush up together,' Nicole said.

That was one thing about Nicole, Amanda thought, admiringly. She could say things like that without blushing or stammering.

As Jim and Nicole stared at each other, Amanda felt suddenly awkward. She looked over at Harrison. He shrugged and smiled. She found herself staring at him. His lips curved appealingly as his smile widened. The right corner lifted a little more than the left, giving him an audacious expression that teased her imagination.

When he moved toward her, Amanda realized that she was still staring at him. Rattled, she turned away abruptly and walked over to the stereo on the credenza behind her desk. Her racing pulse didn't help matters any as she tried to sort through the CDs stacked there.

She sensed him behind her and gripped the lapels of her lab coat as if to protect herself from his presence. She felt his hands on her shoulders and sucked in her breath. Her heart hammered painfully.

'Let me help you off with this,' he

said, next to her ear.

For a pulse-pounding moment, Amanda thought he meant her clothes, then she realized he was referring to her lab coat.

'Oh, thank you,' she managed to mutter. She didn't want to turn around because she knew her face was scarlet.

'I'm afraid we'll only have an hour to practice tonight,' Amanda chattered. She cringed. Her voice was too loud, too nervous sounding. 'Nicole's got — '

'Nothing to do at all!' Nicole finished breathlessly.

'But — ' Amanda whirled to confront her friend.

'So why don't we get started,' Nicole suggested.

'Great idea.' Harrison said.

'Fine.' Amanda shrugged. She might as well get on with step one of the makeover of Harrison Kincaid, she told herself. Just because they were going to be in each other's arms didn't mean she had to get in a tizzy about it.

'I assume you know how to move to

music, but you don't know the formal steps for dances like tango, waltz, and such?' she asked in her most teacherish voice.

'Right. I'm pretty sure I can shake it with the best of them.' Harrison winked, disconcerting Amanda.

Could he really move to the beat? Amanda shuddered, not wanting to see the navy suit and banana yellow shirt grooving to the music. 'Okay. Then at the wedding, the first dance will probably be a waltz. Just watch my feet while I go through the basic steps.'

Slowly, she counted it off, 'One, two, three. One, two, three. One, two, three.' Amanda went through a whole series, then asked him to count with her and follow her steps while she moved around the large room.

After a few minutes, she said, 'Now, I'm going to start the music. Just listen and watch.' She punched the power button on the stereo. The CD she selected was classic Frank Sinatra — slow, romantic songs perfect for dancing.

Intent on what she was doing, she didn't notice Jim Nguyen draw Nicole into his arms and begin waltzing.

'Let's give it a try.' She held out her arms and looked up at him.

Harrison's blood pounded heavily through his veins as he looked at her arms outstretched in welcome. He stepped up to her but held his arms out incorrectly.

Jim Nguyen and Nicole laughed. Amanda frowned at them. 'Not that way, Harrison,' she gently corrected. 'Don't copy me. Do the opposite. You'll be leading, and I'll follow.'

Harrison had to concentrate to complete a maneuver he'd been doing since he was twelve. His mouth felt dry, and his throat felt tight. 'Oh, so that's how it's done.' He swapped arms and pulled her gently, but firmly, into his dancing embrace and nearly sighed at the feel of her in his arms. She just didn't fit well. She fit perfectly.

He looked into her eyes and felt himself falling. He wanted to be closer to her than her stiff dancing posture allowed. For a moment, he forgot what they were supposed to be doing. He stepped forward, not dancing, just moving in on her.

'Owww!' Amanda yelped. She grabbed his forearms and hopped on her left foot.

Appalled, Harrison realized that he had trod on her right foot. 'I'm so sorry.' Red-faced with embarrassment, he apologized again. He hadn't stepped on a girl's foot since cotillion back in eighth grade.

'It's nothing.' Amanda pulled away and limped over to one of the high stools by the sink.

Harrison followed. 'Let me see your foot.'

'No. It's all right.' Amanda seated herself. 'I just need to rest a moment.'

'No,' he argued. 'Let me make sure nothing is broken.'

'Are you a foot doctor in addition to a computer genius?'

He ignored her sarcastic question

and seized her right foot.

Before she could stop him, he'd unlaced her shoe.

'Quit that!' She tried to jerk her foot from his grasp, but he held on firmly. She slapped his hands, but he wouldn't let go.

'Settle down. I just want to make sure your foot's not broken.'

He removed the shoe and set it on the counter next to her. Her foot felt small and dainty in his hands. Her toenails were painted a brilliant scarlet, unlike her fingernails, which were varnished with a clear gloss.

Harrison looked up and lost himself again in her deep blue eyes. He forgot what he was doing. His hand stroked over her nylon-clad foot, massaging gently, relishing the warmth of her skin. He stroked each slender toe and rubbed the pad of his thumb across the scarlet-varnished nails.

The dark centers of Amanda's blue eyes dilated. Harrison's body answered in the age-old response of man to woman.

Amanda stared at him. The minute he'd touched her foot, she'd known this was a big mistake. Something about his hands on her — she shivered. She wanted them in other places than her feet! Oh, dear! This was a colossal mistake — right up there with mistaking poisonous toadstools for edible mushrooms.

His eyes smoldered behind the thick lenses. Without conscious thought, Amanda raised her hands to the black-framed glasses and removed them.

'Can you see without these?' Her voice was a mere whisper in the room. The mellow voice of Frank Sinatra sang of flying to the moon, and Amanda felt she was on that rocket ship with him. That would account for that dizzy feeling that had hit her when she'd seen Harrison's eyes without the camouflage of the glasses.

'I think maybe I can manage,' he said in a tight voice, not breaking eye contact with her.

He had the kind of eyes women called bedroom eyes. That was the only way to describe the incredible, velvet brown eyes that stared back at her. They drew her into their dark depths. The intensity of his gaze made her feel hot and cold, all at the same time. Then she smelled the wonderful scent he wore. It seemed to strengthen with each moment that ticked by.

'You smell wonderful.' She leaned toward him. Without the glasses, he didn't look so bad either. What would he look like with his hair loose and free? Her hands itched to find out.

Harrison took the glasses from her, folded them, and tucked them away in his shirt pocket. Then his hands returned to her injured foot, but his eyes stayed on hers.

If his touch could make her foot feel so much better — kind of tingly and more alive than it had ever felt in all her twenty-eight years — she wondered if he could cure the ache in other parts of her body which suddenly seemed to throb with an intensity that was nearly painful.

'Hey, what's going on over here?' Nicole asked as Jim swirled her to a stop next to them.

Amanda shook herself. Horrified, she felt the blood rush to her face.

'Nothing. Harrison stepped on my foot.' She wasn't attracted to him! She wasn't! Quickly, she pulled her foot free of his grasp. How could she be attracted to him? She looked at his clothes, his hair and decided she must be suffering from some kind of temporary insanity.

'Should I get some ice for it?' Nicole asked.

'No. It's no big deal. It'll be fine. But maybe we should call it quits for tonight.' Amanda reached for her shoe and hurriedly shoved her foot into the ugly thing.

'Oh, do we have to?' Nicole asked, plaintively. 'I mean this is so much fun.'

'Why don't we meet again tomorrow night?' Jim suggested.

'I'm free,' Harrison said.

'Me too,' Nicole said. 'Amanda, I've been thinking. Maybe I'll go to your cousin's wedding after all. I'd forgotten how much fun it is to dance this way. Do you think it's too late for me to change my R.S.V.P. if I call her tonight?'

Amanda gaped at her friend. 'You're not serious? I thought you wouldn't be caught dead there?'

Nicole shrugged. 'I changed my mind. Jim and I were talking about it, and it suddenly sounded like it might be fun. We could make it a foursome.'

'A foursome?' Amanda echoed, thinking things were moving too fast for her to keep up. She laced her shoe and stood, ignoring the slight pain in her foot.

'I just pointed out how much fun it would be for the four of us to go together.' Jim grinned. 'Don't you think, Harrison?'

Harrison's eyes gleamed. 'Oh, definitely.' He turned to look askance at Amanda. 'If that's all right with you, of course.'

'Well, sure. It's okay with me.' At least they wouldn't have to coach Jim on how to dress. 'And I'm sure it will be okay if you call my aunt, Nicole. There's so many people invited that a couple more won't make a difference.'

'Then it's a date,' Nicole chirped.

'Yeah, it sounds like fun,' Jim agreed.

'Sure.' Amanda thought of a great deal more she could say, but she decided to keep it to herself. It sounded like the farthest thing from fun that she could imagine. Yet she found herself thinking that with Harrison with her, it might be bearable.

'So are we on for tomorrow night?' Harrison asked.

Troubled by conflicting emotions, Amanda sighed. 'I guess so.'

'I promise not to step on your feet. In fact, I'll practice everything you showed me tonight. You'll be surprised when you see how much progress I'll have made,' he promised.

'I can hardly wait,' Amanda muttered, leading them toward the front of the store. 'I guess Nicole and I will bid you good night then.'

'Oh, I've decided not to stay after all.' Nicole grasped Jim's arm and pulled him with her. 'We decided to take in the latest Travolta film.'

'We?' Amanda asked. She glared at her friend who waved an airy good-bye.

Her question went unanswered as the other couple left.

Amanda was alone with Harrison Kincaid.

8

Amanda hoped Harrison didn't realize how nervous he made her. 'I think I must have missed something this evening.' Her laugh sounded weak to her own ears.

'It looks as if Nicole and Jim hit it off rather well.' Harrison turned the key in the lock.

'What are you doing?' Amanda's pulse kicked up a notch.

Harrison looked around the show-room. 'I thought maybe you could give me a tour. I'd like to know exactly what a perfumer is or does.'

He swept his arm around the glistening display of colorful bottles arranged on glass shelves. 'Are these some of the brands you sell?'

She relaxed. This was an area that held no uncertainty for her. 'No. Not these. Actually, I design perfumes for individual clients.'

'Scent From Heaven?' He picked up a bottle and noticed that it was empty. 'Clever. How'd you get started?'

'I've mixed up all kinds of concoctions since I was a kid. Before I got my degree in botany, I had planned to teach, but I found myself getting more and more orders for my perfumes. Some kids worked at burger joints. I created and sold perfumes, using my mother's kitchen as my lab.'

'I imagine that must have made your house smell good.'

She laughed. 'That's a matter of opinion. I think my dad got tired of eating meat loaf that smelled like flowers.'

He grimaced. 'That might be a problem.'

'Before it became a problem, Daddy and Uncle Leon, my dad's older brother, said they'd invest in me if I wanted to open a business. Nicole and I had met in college, so she bought an interest in the business too. And here we are.'

'Looks like it was a good investment for them.' He glanced around the elegant salon.

'I'm proud to say it was. Of course, Uncle Leon had just lost Aunt Sally to cancer so it gave him something to get involved with.'

'I'm sorry,' he murmured.

'Thanks. Daddy kind of backed away, and let Uncle Leon be the one I had to call every day for whatever cropped up. I think it helped him get over the loss.'

'Yeah, I just realized recently that it's not good to let someone isolate themselves from life when they lose someone they love.'

'Your mother?' Amanda guessed.

He nodded. 'Just the other night, I suddenly realized that my dad has been gone ten years. Mom, even though she's still young, has never had a date in all that time. Don't get me wrong. I loved my dad and miss him still, but I know that he wouldn't have wanted her to be alone like this.'

'Maybe we can put your mom and

my uncle together,' Amanda joked.

Harrison froze in the act of setting the bottle back on the shelf. 'You know, that might be the answer.'

'The answer to what?'

'Is your uncle still single?'

'Sure. I don't think he's seeing anyone either. He spends most of his time playing golf.'

Harrison smiled broadly. 'We'll talk more about this.' He picked up another bottle. 'Why do these empty bottles have your store label on them?'

Amanda walked to the glass shelves that covered the right side of the room. 'The empty bottles are samples of the different flasks available for clients. I create a perfume for them, and they get to choose their own container. I've got crystal, Venetian glass, and even antique bottles.'

'What are all these different bottles here?' he asked.

'These are collectible perfumes. They're for sale only if I can find a bottle to replace the one I sell.'

'You mean perfumes can be collected like wine or antiques?'

'Something like that, though a perfume is more delicate and more easily ruined than a wine.' She lifted a small bottle with a wooden top. 'Some perfumes aren't made anymore. There are women who will pay practically anything for a bottle of this, for instance.'

Harrison sniffed. 'Um, I like that.'

Amanda smiled. 'Most men seem to. It's Woodhue by Fabergé. Not a terribly expensive perfume when it was mass produced.'

She replaced the bottle in its spot on the shelf and removed a cobalt blue bottle. 'How do you like this?' She removed the top and offered the bottle to him.

'My grandmother had those blue bottles when I was a kid.' Harrison sniffed. 'Very nice, but I don't see why this is any more desirable than anything else. If one perfume isn't available, why not just buy a different one? Perfume is perfume. Just switch brands.'

'Oh, no,' Amanda said earnestly, capping the bottle and replacing it. 'A woman's choice of perfume is a complicated matter.'

He shrugged. 'My mother has worn the same thing as long as I can remember. I figure it's just an ingrained habit.'

Amanda disagreed. 'She wears Chanel No. 5 because something about it speaks to her. It's kind of like picking out art. What is it about a painting that makes one person turn his nose up at it, and another person think he can't live without it?'

Harrison watched as she removed an identical blue bottle and opened it for him to smell.

'It's okay.' He shrugged.

'Selecting a scent is a very personal choice, based on complex psychological stimuli as much as conscious enjoyment of the fragrance. For a woman who identifies with a particular perfume, it feels as if she's lost part of herself when she can no longer acquire it.'

Amanda brought the blue bottle to her nose and smiled. 'Both the blue bottles are Evening in Paris. A whole generation of women grew up wearing it. Then they stopped producing it in the United States, but it's still made in France. I import it for one of my clients.'

'So you locate hard-to-find perfumes for your customers?'

Amanda nodded. 'I don't track them down myself. I use professionals who make it their business to locate so-called lost fragrances. I just kind of stumbled on these' — she waved her hand to encompass the display — 'by accident. I collected them one by one. Before I knew it, I had a little museum here.'

She replaced the bottle. 'This Evening in Paris was made in the United States.'

'Is it my imagination or does it smell a little different from that first blue bottle?'

'Very good!' Amanda eyed him. 'I

must say I'm impressed. Not many people pick up on that. Of course with your dark coloring, maybe it's not that unusual.'

He laughed. 'What have the color of my eyes and my hair got to do with anything?'

'The olfactory region located at the upper end of each nostril' — Amanda touched her nose — 'is yellow in appearance. The darker the shade of yellow, the keener the sense of smell.'

'So you're saying I have a dark yellow olfactory region because I have black hair?' he teased.

'Actually, you're right. Genetics rule. Albinos have limited ability to smell, whereas darker-skinned people smell the most.'

'So I smell the most?'

'Yes.' She blushed. 'I mean — you know what I mean.'

Harrison looked at her. 'But you're a blonde. And you appear to be a natural blonde, so how come your nose is so great?'

She shrugged. 'Just a freak of nature, I guess. It's a proven fact that the darker the person, the darker the olfactory bulb and the better the sense of smell.'

'Sounds like the old schnoz is a lot more complicated than I thought.'

'That's very true.' Amanda warmed to her subject. 'When we are doing something as simple as walking, or eating, or as complex as having sex — ' Amanda broke off. She couldn't believe she'd said that! Where was her brain? Obviously preoccupied with the wrong subject. Her eyes widened as she saw the heat flare in his velvet brown eyes.

'Yes? What happens?' He took a step closer.

Suddenly, she was aware of his own scent. When she got a particularly strong whiff of his cologne, she forgot the horrid clothes he wore and his slicked-down hair. She looked into his sexy eyes, and tried to continue talking, but her voice shook. She turned and grabbed a bottle off the shelf, desperate for something to hold on to.

'With our other senses — our eyes, for instance — a signal is sent to our cerebral cortex where conscious thinking takes place before a signal is then sent to our limbic system.'

'That's quite a mouthful,' he murmured, reaching up and touching her lips with his thumb.

Her mouth fell open. Then it closed. She rushed on. 'But when our olfactory bulb detects odor, the signal goes straight to our limbic system.'

She fell silent as a wave of his scent washed over her. It was as hypnotic as his voice. Her eyes closed, and she felt herself sway. What would he do if she jumped into his arms? Amanda felt as if her heart was going to leap from her chest, it was pounding so hard.

'I imagine sex makes the limbic system go wild, huh?' Harrison asked.

Amanda's eyes snapped open. That audacious smile of his dared her to continue her lecture. She felt every tiny hair on her body rise in expectation.

His scent wafted to her in waves, making her dizzy. She wanted to pull him close and bask in his scent until she figured out what it was.

'It is an act — that is, an event, uh, that creates quite a bit of stimulus.' Her voice quavered. 'Much of which is olfactory.'

'Really? This is fascinating. Do go on.' He stepped even closer.

Breathlessly, she said, 'The limbic system . . . '

He reached out and took the bottle from her hands and replaced it on the shelf. 'I wouldn't want this to slip out of your hands,' he whispered. 'What does the limbic system do?' His voice was hushed, almost mesmerizing.

'It's a mysterious area of the brain.' Amanda fought the desire to let her eyes close. 'Ancient and mysterious,' she babbled. Her hands twisted nervously. 'It's where we feel basic emotions. Like joy.'

'And lust?' he asked, his voice a husky whisper.

She nodded, heart suddenly hammering. 'Yes.' She knew her limbic system was experiencing a tidal wave of lust at the moment. 'Unlike our other senses, smell needs nothing to translate it. We breathe, we smell, boom. It's into the primitive part of our brain. We react.'

'Breathe?' He stepped close and leaned to the curve of her neck and inhaled.

It was all Amanda could do to keep from grabbing him.

'Smell? Um, you're right. I do smell a faint scent of something very appealing,' he murmured.

'But I'm not wearing perfume,' Amanda whispered, swaying beneath an onslaught of an emotion she'd seldom felt in her life. Desire. Sweet, hot desire.

'Boom. We react.' His head lowered. In the last moment before his lips met hers, she whispered, 'I never wear perfume when I'm designing. It interferes with my nose.'

'Amanda?' he whispered, his mouth a

millimeter from hers.

'Yes?' She stared wide-eyed at him.

'Close your eyes and let your limbic system work.'

Then his mouth was on hers, and she couldn't talk. She couldn't think. In fact, it was all she could do to remain standing. She could only feel. And it felt wonderful!

If she'd had any breath left, she'd have sighed in pleasure. His kiss was unlike any she'd experienced before. He shaped her lips with his, molding them, savoring them. Oh, but he could kiss! She'd never have thought a guy who looked like him would even know how to kiss.

His mouth left hers. She sucked in badly needed air and heard his ragged breath as an echo of hers. Amanda reached up and pulled his lips back to hers. She wanted more. It was all she could do to keep from voicing that thought loudly.

Not ready to end the sweet torment, Amanda pressed closer, wanting to feel the length of his body against hers.

A loud crack broke through the sensual fog that enveloped her. Her eyes opened to meet his amused ones.

'What was that?' she whispered.

'Maybe it was the dam breaking on my limbic system,' he suggested.

His teasing words completed the trip back to reality. Face flaming, she hastily released the back of his head and stepped away from him. She was mortified. How could she have made such a spectacle of herself and with such a . . . such a geek, for heaven's sake! She'd have him thinking that she was in love with him if she wasn't careful.

Harrison reached into his coat pocket and removed the black-framed glasses, neatly broken at the bridge into two halves.

'Oh, dear. I'll be glad to pay for them.'

'There's no need.' Harrison studied them. 'Some tape should fix them as good as new.'

Amanda wanted to groan. She supposed she could look forward to him wearing a pair of tape-repaired glasses next time she saw him. If she needed another reminder of his geekiness, he'd just provided her with one.

'I'm sorry for what just happened,' Amanda apologized stiffly. 'I don't know what came over me.'

'Please, no apology is necessary,' Harrison said. 'This subject of the olfactory region and smells is so fascinating that I guess we got carried away.'

'Yes, yes, that was it exactly,' Amanda agreed quickly. 'I was just interested in analyzing your scent. The closer I can get to a smell, the quicker I can discover what it is.' She hoped he believed that bit of idiocy that flew out of her mouth.

'Oh, sure. I understand. I'm the same way when I'm all wrapped up in trying to solve a puzzle. I get carried away and forget where I am, what day it is, or when I last ate.'

Amanda nodded. Sure. That had to be the answer, she rationalized. Maybe she'd been right with her off the wall explanation.

The more she thought about it the more sense it made. It was just her fascination with his scent. It made perfect sense.

Whatever had come over her had faded away. She moved quickly away from him nevertheless, not trusting herself to withstand whatever impulse had propelled her into his arms.

'I'm afraid you need to leave now.' Amanda tried to sound cool and calm, but she felt desperate to be alone. If he left, maybe she could regain her wits.

'Are you certain?'

'Yes. I have, uh, a long day tomorrow,' she babbled, adding other excuses and took a couple of steps away from him for good measure.

'I've really enjoyed the evening. You've really shown me some great moves — for the dance floor.'

Amanda couldn't decide whether he

was teasing or being serious. Since she didn't think geeks behaved like Casanova on the make, she chose to take his words at face value.

'I'm glad you found the lesson beneficial,' she said carefully.

'Oh, it was. I can't wait for the next one.'

Well, all he was going to get next time was a dance lesson, she vowed silently. No more kissing. She definitely did not plan a repeat performance of ending up in his arms.

Amanda made some polite reply as she walked him to the door. This whole incident — she didn't even want to refer to it as The Kiss — must have been some kind of aberration. She just couldn't see herself getting hung up on Harrison Kincaid. He wasn't the kind of man she saw in her future — even though he made her want to kiss him forever.

'Are you sure you don't want me to walk you to your car?' he asked.

'Very sure. I've got some work to

finish up,' she lied. 'I always get someone from mall security to walk me out.'

He nodded. 'Good.'

Amanda clasped her arms together. She felt as if she needed something to hold on to, or she'd fly apart.

'I'll leave then — on one condition.'

'What's that?' she asked warily.

'I'll leave if you'll let me treat you to lunch Friday, at my office. I'll give you the nickel tour.'

'Oh, I don't think so. I have so much work to do.'

'I promise to lecture only on theory, not specifics.' He grinned.

'No, it's not that.' She forced a laugh, unable to tell him that he made her as nervous as the proverbial feline on a very hot tin roof.

'I'd really like to treat you to lunch as a thank you for the dance lessons,' he pleaded. 'Call it an apology for stomping all over your poor foot.'

'That's not necessary,' Amanda assured him. She unlocked the door and held it open, but he didn't move.

'Come on, Amanda. Say yes. Come visit me. I'll let you play with my toys.'

She didn't know how to reply to that! Especially since she couldn't think of any toy of his except the obvious one. Surely he wasn't suggesting . . .

'Virtual reality will be the toy in demand in a few years,' he coaxed. 'I've got one you won't believe.'

'Oh, virtual reality!' She felt like wiping her brow in relief. 'Gee, I don't know, Harrison. I'm so busy. It's just a couple of weeks to Valentine's Day.'

'So you'll be working through lunch?'

'If necessary,' she hedged.

'Cool. I'd love to watch you work. I found our entire discussion about scent extremely educational and interesting. I could bring lunch over here.' He grinned slyly. 'You can teach me more about the limbic system.'

'Maybe I could take off for a late lunch,' Amanda said hurriedly. Being in his office with other employees was preferable to being alone in her lab with him. 'Say one-thirty?'

'Great. I can promise you it'll be interesting.' Harrison walked through the doorway. 'See you tomorrow night for our next lesson.'

'I'll be here.' Amanda sighed dolefully.

On the one hand, she mused, watching him walk away, he made her cringe each time she looked at him. On the other hand, there was something about him that made her go weak in the knees after she'd been around him a few minutes.

Amanda couldn't bear to think about what that might mean.

*   *   *

The phone was ringing when Harrison walked into his condo. He picked up the cordless from the kitchen counter. 'Yeah, Mom?' he asked, knowing it had to be her.

'Well? Tell me,' Lynn Kincaid squealed. 'How did it go?'

Harrison gave her a carefully edited version of the night's events while he walked to the living room. He'd have to figure out a way to explain to her his reasons for dressing like the ultimate nerd. Maybe by the weekend, he would have let Amanda transform him so wardrobe wouldn't be a continuing problem.

'I still don't understand why you let her think you can't dance.'

'It's just a little joke, Mom. Besides, it gives me an excuse to hold her in my arms,' he teased, dropping onto the buff leather couch.

'Harrison! That's awful.' Yet she giggled.

When he told her that he was seeing Amanda again the next night and then taking her to lunch and giving her a tour of his offices on Friday, he knew she was pleased.

'You know, Mom. This time you didn't do so bad.'

Harrison thought about the way he'd felt when Amanda had kissed him and clung to him, pleading without words for more. He'd love to have complied with her silent request if only his glasses hadn't seized that moment to loudly snap in two.

He fell silent, listening to his mother chatter on about something or other. He'd be willing to bet that Amanda had forgotten all about his geeky appearance when she'd been in his arms. Was it possible for a geek to win the heart of a beauty like Amanda?

That question startled him. He didn't want to win her heart, did he? He just wanted to have some fun with her before moving on. That was all he wanted, wasn't it? He thrust the disturbing thoughts away.

Inspired, he asked, 'Mom, why don't you have dinner with Amanda and me this weekend?'

'Oh, no. I would just be a fifth wheel.'

Not if he had anything to say about it. Harrison used all his charm to get her to agree to meeting them at his condo for dinner. He could kill two birds with one stone that way — get his mother and Amanda's uncle together and get Amanda into the more personal setting of his home. Either way, he was certain something positive was bound to come of the evening.

When his mother said good night, he replaced the phone and lay back on the couch, hands clasped behind his head. He stared at the ceiling thoughtfully as if the answers to the disturbing questions were written on the stucco-like texture.

The phone rang again, interrupting his reverie. He grinned when he heard Jim's voice.

'So you liked Nicole?' Harrison asked, feeling rather smug.

'She's a pistol!' Jim said. 'I don't think I've ever laughed so much — with a woman, that is.'

'Can I pick them or can I pick them?'

'Yeah, I noticed the one you picked out for yourself is really something. Don't know if I'd want the hassles of dating a beautiful woman. My Nicole is perfect — sexy as all get out, cute, and appealing.'

'Your Nicole?' Harrison asked, bemused.

'Well, yeah,' Jim said diffidently. 'So?'

'Nothing. Nothing.' Harrison was glad Jim couldn't see his wide grin. 'But what do you mean about the hassles of dating a beautiful woman?'

'You know. Guys hitting on her all the time. Always having to tell her she's beautiful — like she can't look in a mirror and see. And if you date her, you always have to look like you just stepped out of a Calvin Klein commercial. Beautiful women are high maintenance. Definitely not my mug of beer.'

Harrison laughed. 'Well, you're wrong about Amanda. I don't think she's like that at all. As to my having to look good when seen with her, you're way off. You saw how I was dressed.'

'Yeah. You didn't tell me tonight was a costume party.' Jim laughed. 'When I saw you in that get-up, I was so sorry

I didn't have my camera.'

'Now you know why I didn't mention it in advance. I'd probably have seen that photo on the bulletin board in the break room,' Harrison said.

'Damn straight! What was that all about anyway?'

'It started out innocently enough.' Harrison sighed. 'Then it got complicated.'

'It always does when it involves a woman,' Jim said. 'So tell me.'

'I just wanted to make sure my mom's latest blind date would reject me. I didn't want to go out with her, but I didn't want to hurt her feelings either. I figured Amanda would be like all the other women my mom has thrown at me.'

Jim whistled. 'There's nothing remotely canine about Amanda. And she's way better than that snooty lawyer with the fake British accent you dated last year. So why would she even need a date? Doesn't she have a steady guy?'

'She couldn't have.' Worry pricked

him. Could she? Harrison's forehead wrinkled. 'I haven't figured out why a woman like her agreed to a blind date in the first place.'

'I can't see why on earth she'd give you the time of day, but I can sure understand your attraction to her — beyond the obvious, that is. She's a mystery wrapped in an enigma, or something like that.'

'Winston Churchill might have characterized Russia that way,' Harrison said dryly, 'but I think it's a little much to say the same about Amanda. I don't think she's quite that complicated.'

So far, he'd had a heck of a good time trying to figure her out. It came as a pleasant surprise that she had such a compassionate nature. When Jim had laughed at him, Amanda had been understanding and soothing — gentle in her explanations. And she was obviously intelligent.

They talked on, and Harrison told Jim about his date with Amanda for a tour of the company on Friday.

Jim laughed. 'Maybe I'll ask Nicole over too.'

'Get your own lunch then. I want Amanda all to myself without her friend running interference. Things get real interesting when she's alone with me.'

'I just bet they do.' Jim guffawed.

After a bit, Harrison hung up and resumed staring at the living room ceiling. He could hardly wait to see Amanda again. In fact, it was all he could do not to call her, just to hear her voice. He much preferred her soft Texas drawl to Marcy's pseudo-British accent.

With a smile, he visualized their next encounter. Wouldn't Amanda be surprised when she saw how much his dancing had improved?

9

'Nicole, if you desert me tonight, I'll never speak to you again.' Amanda paced around the lab, stopping at her desk. She grabbed the art samples for her Valentine's ad and stared at them, not really seeing the red hearts. 'He's late.'

Nicole glanced at her watch. 'Only by thirty seconds.' She sighed. 'Why do I have to chaperone you? You're a big girl.'

'I need protection.'

'Protection? From Harrison? Not really. He seems like such a nice guy.'

'He is.'

Nicole walked over to Amanda and grabbed her arm. 'Wait a minute. You're not making sense. If he's a nice guy, why do you need protection?'

'From myself! Not from him!' Amanda pulled away from her friend.

At Nicole's bewildered look, Amanda continued. 'This is all your fault, Nicole!' Agitated, she slapped the sample art pages against her hand as she paced.

'My fault?' Nicole yelped. 'What's my fault? Wait a minute! Are you saying that you can't trust yourself alone with Harrison?'

'That's exactly what I'm saying.'

Stunned, Nicole sank onto the armchair in front of Amanda's desk. 'Whew! I don't believe this. You mean he turns you on?'

'No. But — '

'But?'

'It's just that things happen when we're together. Alone.'

'Geez, this is unbelievable. He really does turn you on?'

'Call it what you want, I just don't want to be alone with him.'

Nicole planted her fisted hands on her hips. 'So it finally happened.'

'What are you talking about? What happened?'

'You finally found a guy who ignored that Do Not Disturb sign.'

Amanda fidgeted beneath her scrutiny.

'Am I right?'

'I don't know what you're talking about,' Amanda muttered, studying her fingernails as if their condition was of prime importance.

'Oh, yes, you know very well what I'm talking about. Tell me every juicy detail.'

'There's nothing to tell. I just want you to stay here tonight and not sneak off to the movies or wherever you went last night.'

'We went to the movies,' Nicole protested.

'Sure you did. You've got that I'm-in-love look all over you,' Amanda said.

'And you don't?' Nicole laughed. 'Take a good look in the mirror.'

'I'm not in love with him. Okay, okay. I'll go so far as to admit that maybe — maybe, mind you — Harrison excites me a little. There, are you happy now?' Amanda scowled.

Nicole grimaced. 'Well, apparently, I'm happier than you are about it.'

'You've seen him. How could I possibly be in lo — , I mean excited, even a little, by someone who wears polyester?' Amanda wailed.

'Hey, it's not the end of the world.'

'Oh, easy for you to say. Your new boyfriend looks like a male model. And my new boyfriend — if I could be so bold as to call him that — looks like he's auditioning for a disco nostalgia movie,' she said gloomily. 'In Salvation Army costumes.'

'At least you've got a boyfriend now,' Nicole ventured, not doing a very good job of hiding her smile. 'It's not like that song we sang in kindergarten. First comes love, then comes marriage. First comes boyfriend. Then the rest of it arrives on schedule.'

'Don't be ridiculous. I'm not in love with him. I'm just . . . just confused by him.'

'I'll say.' Nicole walked over to Amanda's desk and grabbed some more of the candy hearts from the bowl.

'Since this is all your fault, I don't think I'd laugh if I were you.' Amanda wadded up the pages and stuffed them in the pocket of her lab coat.

'How do you figure it's my fault?'

'Because if you hadn't said he was my best bet, I wouldn't be in this predicament.'

'Why is liking him a predicament? Or loving him if it comes down to that?'

Amanda ignored her question. She unbuttoned her lab coat and removed it.

Nicole calmly waited for her to answer.

'If you hadn't said we could make him over, I'd never have agreed to dating him. Then this wouldn't have happened.' Amanda slipped the coat on again and began buttoning it.

'Tell me what happened. What are you so excited about?'

Amanda stopped and looked down at her hands as if confused. She began unbuttoning the coat again and removed it.

'Geez, would you stop with the coat!' Nicole grabbed the garment from Amanda's hands.

'After you left last night, Harrison and I . . . it was all perfectly innocent,' Amanda mumbled, not looking at her friend.

'What was?' Nicole asked, frowning.

'Well, I don't know how it happened. I was telling him about how the sense of smell works, and his scent just kept washing over me in waves.'

Nicole's frown deepened. 'Amanda. I'm telling you again. He hasn't worn aftershave any of the times we've seen him. You're imagining things.'

'No. I never hallucinate with my nose. He has this scent that just makes me feel all melting and hot and — ' Amanda broke off. Her face was as red as the Valentine graphics she'd been looking at on the art samples.

'So. What did happen last night?' Nicole demanded, sitting up straighter.

'Well, he kind of — we kind of — ' Amanda mumbled, not daring to look at her friend.

'What?' Nicole yelled. 'You're driving me nuts. What did you do?'

'Kissed.'

'Kissed? You and Harrison? Wait a minute. What do you mean kind of? Did you or didn't you?'

Amanda smiled softly remembering the kiss. 'Oh, we did. Definitely, positively. And what a kiss!'

Nicole shrieked and jumped up and down. 'You kissed the geek.'

'Don't call him that,' Amanda said sharply.

Nicole cocked her head to the right. 'Wait a minute. If you kissed, and judging by the expression on your face, it wasn't horrible, then why don't you want to be alone with him tonight?'

'I just don't. I mean he's nice, and smart, and I like him, and he's a great kisser, but I can't fall for him. I haven't fallen for him. I won't fall for him.'

'Who are you trying to convince? Me or you?' Nicole studied her intently.

'I mean he's a geek, for heaven's sake. Even if we clean him up for Marcy's wedding, he'll still be a geek,' Amanda protested. 'So be a pal and stay tonight,' she pleaded. 'If you're here, he won't be able to talk me into other things.'

'Other things? This gets more and more interesting. Like what?'

'Last night before he left, somehow he persuaded me to have lunch with him Friday.'

'Oh, my! Out in public? How could you withstand the embarrassment of being seen with him?' Nicole clapped a hand on either side of her face in mock horror.

'I can do without your sarcasm. I'm not ashamed to be seen with him.' But her conscience nagged at her. She just couldn't imagine introducing him to her mother and father looking the way he looked tonight. And the thought of going through a reception line at Marcy's wedding with Harrison in a plaid polyester suit was enough to give her an ulcer.

'Are you sure about that?'

Amanda decided not to tell her that lunch would probably be a sandwich at his company's office.

'Nicole, I'm just asking you to please save me from myself. No matter what happens. Don't leave the boutique with Jim tonight.'

Nicole sighed. 'Okay. I guess that's what friends are for. Even when certain other friends are being as dumb as a post.'

'We just don't have anything in common, so why get something going that won't lead to anything?'

'Yeah, I guess you're right. After all, why take chances?'

★ ★ ★

Nicole's comments haunted Amanda. She tried her best not to think of

Harrison, but it was difficult when the object of that conversation was holding her in his arms. And his arms felt very strong and muscular, she suddenly realized.

As equally amazing as his unexpected biceps was the swift progress he'd made as her pupil. Maybe she was a better teacher than she had thought.

'I can't believe how well you're dancing!' she exclaimed.

'Like I say, you're a great teacher.' Harrison changed direction and whirled her around. 'I have a confession to make.' He grinned and winked at her.

'Yes?' She found herself flushing with pleasure at his compliment. That was all it was. Not the sexy wink. Not the closeness of his body. Definitely not that darned scent that still tantalized her. 'What do you confess?'

'I've been practicing.' He grabbed her and dipped her low.

'Oh!' Amanda had a tough time keeping her balance — not to mention her breath. After a few minutes in his

146

arms, she felt as if she had run a marathon. She'd ceased to notice his ugly clothes — the blue suit was paired with a hot pink shirt tonight. At least he wasn't wearing those horrible glasses. Except that made his eyes too accessible to her.

When she forgot about how jittery he made her, Harrison was witty and as much fun to be with as any of her male friends. It wasn't his fault that he also excited her far more than any other man she'd known.

After several turns around the floor, Amanda relaxed and began to enjoy herself. She felt as if she could waltz all night — especially since she'd scorned the ugly black shoes tonight and wore a pair of comfortable pumps instead. She smiled.

'Nicole and I are going to sit this one out,' Jim called out, breaking her reverie.

The music ended, and Harrison twirled her to a stop. To her consternation, she realized she could see the pulse throbbing in his throat. The tanned column of his neck suddenly seemed irresistible. What would he taste like if she covered that fluttering pulse point with her mouth?

Her eyes rounded. What was wrong with her? Hurriedly, she stepped out of his arms. 'How about something cold to drink?'

They all agreed that a Coke would hit the spot.

'Let me help you,' Nicole said.

They went to the tiny kitchen off the lab. Amanda closed the door. She leaned against the door and practiced deep breathing, hoping it would help her jangled nerves. Maybe she needed a vacation.

'Now remember, don't leave tonight,' she reminded Nicole.

Nicole removed four soft drinks from the small fridge. 'Do we have to go through this again?'

'No, I guess not.' Amanda got glasses from the cupboard and filled them with ice. 'Do you think it's too early in our so-called relationship to mention Harrison's clothes?'

Nicole's brow wrinkled in thought. 'Well, you don't have that much time. The wedding is a week from Saturday.'

Amanda pulled the tabs on the cans. The quiet hiss was the only sound in the room as the two women plotted.

'Yeah, let's go ahead and mention it,' Nicole said.

'I still don't know how to work it into a conversation. I can't just say, 'Oh, excuse me, Harrison, but you dress like a real dork. Why don't you let me take you shopping?''

Giggling, Nicole got a tray from the top of the fridge. 'Well, that would be the direct way, but maybe we can figure out something more diplomatic. Just leave it to me.'

'Now I'm really worried.' Amanda took the tray and sighed. 'I'm going to have gray hair by the time this is over. Open the door. I'm ready.'

Harrison hurried over and took the tray from her.

'Thank you,' she murmured, gesturing for him to set it on the long counter.

When they'd quenched their thirst, Nicole said, 'Jim, that's a lovely shirt you have on tonight.'

'Thanks.' Jim shrugged. 'It's just a white shirt.'

'Why, yes, but it is particularly attractive,' Amanda added. 'Where do you shop?'

'The same places everyone else shops — department stores, some of the men's specialty clothing stores.'

Amanda took a big gulp of her soda and prayed for courage. 'That style would look great on you, Harrison. Against your tan.'

'You think so?' Harrison tried to look serious. 'I don't know. I kind of like things with some color.'

Amanda coughed. Yeah, he wore so much color you needed sunglasses when you looked at him. 'Well, color is nice, but there's just something about a dark, well-cut suit and a crisp white shirt — '

'That just makes a woman hot,' Nicole threw in.

'What!' Amanda yelped. She was going to buy a muzzle for Nicole.

Jim saved the day. 'Are you saying I make you hot, Nicole?' he teased.

Amanda didn't hear her friend's murmured reply. Hesitantly, she looked at Harrison.

'So I don't make you hot dressed like this?' he asked, his voice carefully neutral.

Hot? Oh, yeah. If he made her any hotter, she'd burst into flame like flash paper. But she couldn't tell him that.

'Well,' she parried, 'the way you dress is very,' — she hesitated, searching for the right word — 'interesting,' she finally said.

He looked slightly disgruntled at her choice of adjectives so she hurried to add, 'Since I'm not looking for a meaningful relationship, maybe I'm not the one to judge what constitutes hot. Though I agree with Nicole that attractive clothes are, uh, much more attractive — to most women, that is.'

'Interesting? I don't think any man would choose interesting over hot.' He stroked his chin as if in deep thought. It seemed to him as if she'd been plenty hot last night.

'So you're not interested in a romance, or rather, a meaningful relationship with me?' he asked, studying her face as if it were a truth barometer.

Amanda seemed to force her reply out. 'No. I'm not.' She raised her glass to her lips.

Harrison grinned. She'd never pass a lie detector test. 'Then I guess we'll just have to settle for a superficial relationship of lust and sex.'

10

Amanda choked, spewing soda from her mouth. She coughed and turned red in the face and coughed some more.

Harrison rubbed her back, adding to her discomfort by his touch which she felt all the way to her feet. In fact, her toes were probably curling in ecstasy.

'What did you say?' she wheezed.

'I said we'll have a superficial relationship of just plain jests.' He smiled and gave her a look of wide-eyed innocence.

Amanda was ninety percent certain that wasn't what he'd said — unless her hearing had been distorted by wishful thinking. Either way, she decided not to argue the point.

'Are you all right?' Nicole asked.

'Went down the wrong way,' Harrison

said. 'She'll be all right in a minute.' He rubbed her back some more. She squirmed away from his hands.

'Hey, I've got a great idea,' Nicole said. 'Why don't we all go shopping together Saturday.'

'No,' Amanda wheezed. 'I don't think I can make it.' This whole thing was getting out of hand.

'Sure you can. You don't have anything else to do,' Nicole said.

A muzzle was definitely indicated for Nicole.

'I don't have any plans.' Jim pointed at Nicole. 'You're elected to help me pick out a new cummerbund and bow tie for the wedding. We can match it to the color of your dress.'

'Cool!' Nicole said

'You really are going to the wedding with Nicole?' Amanda asked, finally getting her voice back to normal.

'Sure. Sounds like fun.'

'Yes, shopping and lunch Saturday do sound like fun,' Harrison said.

For Amanda's ears only, he added,

'You can help me pick out some of those clothes that make a woman hot. Not that they'd work on you, of course, but I might get lucky with someone else.'

'Not if I have anything to say about it.' The words slipped out of her mouth.

'What did you say?' Harrison asked.

'I said, uh, hot — if I have any ginseng about,' Amanda improvised. 'I meant if I've got any ginseng, I can make you a cologne that will really be hot. Ginseng is prized as an aphrodisiac in some cultures, you know.'

'Oh. Okay. Make me up a barrel. And don't worry, Amanda,' he said. 'Even if I get lucky, I'll still escort you to your cousin's wedding.'

'Thanks so much.' Amanda said with saccharine sweetness. How had he gone from kissing her to requesting her help in making other women hot in a nanosecond?

She'd make him some cologne all right. Just as soon as she went to the woods and gathered some poison ivy.

She had this terrible suspicion that Harrison was just like all the other men she'd met. He was falling head over heels into like with her.

Harrison set his empty glass on the tray. 'Okay. I've got my second wind. I'm ready to dance. Let's try something different this time,' he suggested.

'Good idea.' Jim pulled Nicole close. 'I'm for something a little different.'

'What did you have in mind?' Amanda asked.

'How about a tango?' Harrison said.

A shiver slithered up Amanda's spine. She had to clear her throat to speak. 'Sure. No problem.' She cleared her throat again. 'But it's kind of a complicated dance. You might want to wait before adding more dance steps to your repertoire.'

Harrison grinned. 'I have another confession to make.'

'I can hardly wait,' Amanda muttered.

'I checked out a dance tape at the video store last night and practiced for hours. I think I can manage the steps.'

Suddenly, it seemed as if there wasn't enough oxygen in the room. A fine tremor shook her hands as she shuffled through the CDs, looking for appropriate music. She took a deep breath and popped her choice, sultry Latin music, into the stereo and turned up the volume a little. She didn't want the music soft and seductive. That way lay temptation.

The strains of guitar accompanied by a throbbing conga drum reverberated through the suddenly too-quiet room.

Harrison clicked his heels together and straightened up in the required haughty posture. He beckoned imperiously for Amanda. Oh, my! He had the moves down perfectly. Her heartbeat picked up in time to the conga drum.

Amanda felt like calling out for help. But when she turned her head, she saw Nicole and Jim sneak through the door leading from the lab to Nicole's office. *Why, you little traitor*, she thought, knowing Nicole was taking Jim to her own office for some serious smooching.

Just then Harrison touched her hand. Amanda turned to face him in a dancer's pose. When he swept her into his arms, she nearly stumbled but recovered quickly.

Determined to resist him, she tried to make conversation. 'How did Nicole and Jim become a couple so quickly,' she gasped, as he pulled her close. She would not allow herself to be affected by the music or by the heat in his eyes. Amanda shivered. Pure heat.

'I guess they're just lucky,' he answered, taking a sweeping step forward.

Amanda stumbled over her own feet. 'Sorry.' She was having a hard time following his dramatic moves.

'Instant rapport is what it is, I guess.' He snapped his head to the right and lunged that way.

She didn't bother to retort that instant lust was more like it, judging by the way the two had looked at each other from the moment they had met.

Instinctively, Amanda knew just saying the word *lust* was playing with fire. Better not to mention anything to do with the subject. Especially when she still felt the effects of her last experience. On the other hand, Harrison didn't seem to feel anything weird happening between them. Maybe he didn't feel anything at all.

Instant lust or love at first sight was just chemical attraction, she knew. Male and female pheromones. That's what Nicole and Jim were responding to. That was the same problem that plagued her, she realized.

For some reason, her pheromone receptors reacted with extraordinary sensitivity to Harrison's pheromones. She knew exactly what it was, but it seemed to be beyond her ability to control.

What she needed was a good head cold. That would put an end to this love-at-first-sight syndrome. *Love at first sight?* She tripped over her own feet.

'Want to take a breather?' Harrison asked.

'No!' Dancing with him was safer than standing still, alone with him.

'I found our conversation last night fascinating.' Harrison drew Amanda closer to him.

She felt the heat of his skin as her cheek grazed his as they alternated side to side. She was so overpowered by him — by everything about him — that she didn't even find his ability to dance a sensual tango so astonishing.

'In fact,' he continued, keeping her close to him, 'I did a little Internet research about the matter.'

Harrison didn't even seem out of breath, but she could hardly find enough oxygen in the room to keep going.

'I read that smell triggers memories because there is no short term memory where smell is concerned. It's all long term. Smells remain with us for all our lives.'

Amanda didn't want to get onto the

subject of smell. Last night, after he'd left, was when she'd first begun to think about this matter of smell and phero-mones. It certainly explained why she reacted so strongly to his scent — a scent no one else seemed to be aware of. She could only wonder if he picked up any kind of female pheromone from her. If he did, he didn't seem overwhelmed by it, she thought, rather disgruntled about the fact.

'You've told me that I have a special scent,' Harrison said.

'Oh, that. I was mistaken,' Amanda said, reluctant to discuss his appealing scent. 'Let me tell you instead about how I design perfumes for women who want their own individual fragrance.'

Harrison smiled. 'Tell me. I find this entire business fascinating.'

'It's endlessly fascinating.' Amanda plastered a cheerful grin on her face. 'Right now, as I told you, I'm working on special orders for Valentine's Day. That's one of the most romantic occasions and most profitable for me.

It's right up there with Christmas.'

'What does a gentleman get a lady like you for Valentine's Day?' he interjected. 'I imagine you're bored with the same old heart-shaped box of candy year in and year out.'

Amanda's fake smile faded. Her eyes dropped. It pained her to admit she'd never had one of those gaudy red boxes. 'Oh, diamonds, emeralds, rubies — some little bauble like that,' she said airily to hide her hurt.

Harrison felt the tension in her body as she'd answered his question. He imagined her wearing gifts like that — and nothing else. Rubies at her ears. Emeralds on her wrist. A diamond on her ring finger. The thought didn't even frighten him. Instead, he felt a strange tightness and heat inside him at the thought of her wearing his badge of ownership. Call him a throwback, but he kind of liked the idea of her belonging only to him.

Harrison studied Amanda. That was the bad thing about blondes — at least this blonde. He'd learned to read her already. When she was upset, she always blushed. And she was blushing now. He suspected that she was joking about the Valentine gifts. But surely she'd received her fair share of those corny items in years past. If she hadn't, then that made no sense, but it gave him plenty of food for thought.

'Go on and tell me about how you design a fragrance,' he encouraged, knowing she'd relax when she started talking about her work.

'The client selects a bottle from the ones in the showroom.'

'Looks like you've got quite a collection to choose from.'

Amanda nodded. 'Then the client decides whether the scent is to be splashed on or sprayed in an atomizer. They fill out a questionnaire and write a little profile of the person who is to receive the perfume. I take that and create something which represents that person.'

'You mean if they're athletic or

whatever?' He noticed the way she relaxed when she talked about her work.

'Exactly. I try to match the perfume to the person, based upon their personality, their likes and dislikes of certain aromas, and their lifestyle.'

'Wow. I'm impressed. Do you use a computer to help you?'

'No way. I use my nose.'

'There are computers that can analyze scents,' he teased.

'I know but this isn't a forensics lab. This is — ' She looked sheepish. 'I started to say magic. I hate to say it because it sounds ridiculous, but I think of making perfume as alchemy. It is nearly a magical process.' She laughed up at him. 'I know that sounds ridiculous.'

'No. Not at all.' He smiled at her. 'I bet you're very good at your work.'

'I take my work very seriously and very personally.'

'Maybe I will retain you to design a cologne for me so I'll have to beat the women off with a stick when I escort you to your cousin's wedding.'

'You don't need one. Believe me,' Amanda muttered.

Though her voice was low, he heard her. So he was getting to her, he thought satisfied. Geek image and all. 'One thing I've noticed. You don't seem to wear perfume. Yet there always seems to be a fragrance about you. It's rather pleasant, but I can't put my finger on it. What is it?'

Amanda could have told him the same thing. She could have told him what it was also, but she didn't want to believe her own theory. Yet, she couldn't help but wonder if the scent he got from her was as arresting and alluring to him as his was to her.

'I don't wear a scent when I'm working, because it would conflict with whatever mix I was putting together. I'd have a hard time creating a perfume if my smell kept invading my nose.'

'So you told me. Just how did you get into this?'

The music ended, but Harrison kept dancing her around the room.

'I've always had a keen nose, but I guess my interest in scent began at scout camp. One year I took this session where we made our own toiletries — you know, shampoo, hand lotion, and such — from vegetables and fruits. It was fascinating. Then in high school, my interest got another boost in world history. I'm probably one of the few kids who loved learning about the past, especially the medieval and renaissance periods when potions came into their own. You could get something to make you smell good and enchant others at the same time.'

'I read that smells influence us on a biological level, producing hormonal changes in people. Even smelling flowers can excite people.' Harrison led her over to the chairs by her desk.

'Does that surprise you?' she asked. 'The fragrance of a flower is an announcement that it's fertile and that its sex organs — ' Amanda's voice

166

faltered. Suddenly she realized that she'd forgotten to be restrained. She shouldn't even think the word sex either when Harrison was around.

'Yes? Go on,' Harrison encouraged. He stopped his dance movements but didn't release her. When he sank onto one of the chairs, she allowed him to pull her to him as if he were reeling her in on a taut line.

'What were you saying about flowers?' he murmured, looking up at her.

'The flowers . . . they're dripping with nectar. Just waiting to be pollinated.'

'I never thought of flowers as having sex organs.'

Harrison's voice seemed huskier. His gaze intensified, making Amanda feel as if he could see her very thoughts. Her eyelids felt heavy. Maybe she should close them and lean against him for a while.

'Everything has a sex organ, doesn't it?' Amanda felt oddly breathless, as if she were discussing something much more provocative than the sexuality of flowers.

Harrison tugged on her hand, and Amanda jerked closer to him, standing between his wide-spread legs. He dropped her hand and gathered a handful of her black skirt. He felt as if he'd like to do a little pollinating of his own. He looked into her eyes. *Make that a lot of pollinating*, he thought, drawing a ragged breath.

Amanda didn't dare look into his eyes. Her gaze dropped then she blushed scarlet. Her eyes widened at what she saw then jerked upward from their fascinating study. 'Smell is the only sense without which — that we are never without,' she babbled.

Her hands reached up and covered his eyes. 'You can close your eyes and stop seeing.'

Harrison thought he would explode or expire, he wasn't certain which, when she'd touched him.

Her hands moved to his ears. 'You can close your ears and stop hearing.'

He wondered if she could feel the blood pounding in his ears like a big bass drum.

Gracefully, her hands slid down and cupped each of his hands. 'You can refrain from touching and stop feeling.'

He bit back the groan that rose in his throat. He wanted to feel, to touch, to see. To smell.

'But,' she whispered, 'you can't ever close your nose to stop smelling. Without breath, we die.'

'I feel like I'm about to die right now,' he said, strain evident in his voice.

'With breath, we smell — with every inhalation,' Amanda whispered edging closer.

'Excuse us for busting up this purely scientific discussion,' Nicole called from the doorway.

Amanda jumped away from Harrison as if he had barked at her.

'Nicole. I didn't hear you come in.' She hoped her face wasn't as red as it felt.

'Obviously,' Nicole said dryly. 'Jim

left when I told him I had made plans with you for the evening.'

'Plans?' Amanda looked confused.

'Remember. You made me promise to — ?'

Amanda looked panic-stricken, suddenly remembering.

'To go shopping with you,' Nicole finished, grinning impishly.

'Oh, that.' Amanda smoothed over her skirt.

'And I'm not taking no for an answer. Remember?'

'Yes. Of course.' Amanda knew she should be glad that Nicole had interrupted them. Especially when she knew that she had been a breath away from giving Harrison a demonstration of a different way to explore the sense of smell — by kissing him within an inch of his life. But she wasn't glad. Perversely, she wished Nicole had disregarded her duty.

'Well, I guess I need to leave then,' Harrison said easily, but the look he gave Amanda was full of promise. He reached into his shirt pocket and pulled out his glasses. He'd repaired the broken nose piece with white adhesive tape.

'Until tomorrow, Amanda.' He put on the glasses.

She nodded, staring at the picture he made. Somehow she'd get out of her lunch date with him. She had to. Each time she saw him, she found herself slipping more and more under his spell.

She engraved his image on her brain, trying to remind herself that he was completely unacceptable in the looks department. Especially those glasses. She should feel scornful, but all she could feel was the memory of how hard her pulse had pounded when she'd pressed against his body, breaking the glasses. His kiss had been sweeter — and hotter — than any of the candy hearts in the dish on her desk.

If Nicole had been just a minute late in her interruption, she'd have found Amanda and Harrison locked in a kiss so hot it would have singed the air, Amanda thought wistfully.

What was she going to do? She had a sinking feeling that she had fallen in love with him!

11

Amanda felt positively schizophrenic as she checked her appearance in the visor mirror. On one hand she wanted to look her best. On the other, she knew she shouldn't want to impress Harrison. Yet, her heart pounded at the prospect of seeing him.

It was just anxiety because he made her nervous, she kept telling herself, unwilling to admit that excitement suffused her entire being just at the thought of seeing him.

'You are not excited, Amanda Whitfield. And you are definitely not falling in love with him,' she told her bright-eyed reflection. She certainly had no need of blusher today. She pressed her cold hands to her hot cheeks to cool them.

When she opened the door of her Corvette, wind gripped it and almost pulled it from her grasp. She slammed it, set the alarm, and hurried up the walk toward the mirrored-glass building. Her reflection and that of swaying pine trees bounced back to her.

Amanda had done her best to cancel the lunch. She'd called him at one and told him that she was embroiled in a meeting. He'd calmly told her to finish her meeting then come over.

She'd called back at two and tried to cancel again. Harrison had replied that he'd postpone the meal another hour. Then at three, when she'd called again to weasel out, he'd somehow talked her into coming at four o'clock. The guy might be a geek, but he was a silver-tongued geek.

Thus, she found herself arriving at four o'clock for a lunch she was far too nervous to eat. She'd begged and pleaded with Nicole to go with her, but Nicole had just laughed at her and told her to grow up.

Amanda shivered and pulled her winter white coat tighter around the matching dress. She'd just go up, have a sandwich, and leave, she decided, pushing at the revolving door.

A security guard on the other side of the door pushed, speeding her entry through the door. 'Miss Whitfield?'

'Yes, I'm Amanda Whitfield.'

'We've been expecting you. Come right over here and sign in please.' He led her to another security guard at a curved desk. 'Charlie, this is Miss Whitfield.'

'Nice to meet you.' Charlie tipped his hat. 'Top floor. Harrison is expecting you.'

Amanda nodded, slightly dazed at the celebrity treatment. Had Harrison told everyone in the building about their lunch date? Both guards, to her amusement, escorted her to the elevator. One even pushed the button for her, then stepped out, leaving her to ride alone to the tenth floor.

When the elevator doors opened on the top floor, Amanda faced a paneled wall adorned by a starburst design of antique brass displaying the name of Harrison's company in a simple lettering style — *Kincaid Technology*.

She stepped out onto plush amber carpet. To her right was a large door with an electronic card lock on it and to the left was a modern chrome and oak reception desk. It was all very new looking, not ultraexpensive, but not cheap by any means.

The deep pile muffled her footsteps as she approached the receptionist's desk. She was amused to see the old-fashioned lace doily red hearts taped to the front of the desk.

No one was there. There were two doors behind the desk. Both doors had the same slide card locks and also looked as if they had been sound-proofed.

Amanda waited a moment, then called out. 'Hello? Anyone here?' She waited another long moment, fighting the urge to flee.

Just then the door to her left opened. 'Hey, I hope you haven't been waiting long.' Harrison stopped still and looked her up and down. 'Wow! You look sensational.'

If there was one thing she wished she could control, it was the blush response that seemed to work overtime when she was around Harrison. At the moment, she knew her face was as red as the lacy Valentine hearts on the desk.

'Thank you,' Amanda replied, wishing she could return the compliment. She gulped. He wore the hideous blue and orange plaid again. It must be his favorite suit, or he had a very limited wardrobe. At least he'd removed the coat. She sighed. The wet look still reigned supreme. Water dripped from his hair.

Harrison wiped a drop from his forehead. He'd intended for her to see him as he really was today. Plain old Harrison Kincaid — regular clothes, real hair, no glasses. It would have been ridiculous for him to perpetuate this charade with the whole crew here. In fact, he was relieved that he'd have to be honest with her. But Amanda had arrived so late that the office staff was gone.

So, at the last minute, after everyone had left to start the weekend early, he'd chickened out. He felt like a damn fool as he'd hurried to put on his disguise, but he didn't feel secure enough in his relationship with Amanda to risk revealing the truth. What if she told him to get lost? He just couldn't take that chance. He was trapped like the rat he was.

'Uh, I can't stay long,' Amanda hurried to say, eager to let him know she intended to make a quick departure.

'Oh, I'm sorry to hear that.'

Amanda felt guilty at her subterfuge, but it was the only way to save herself.

'Well, do you want to eat first or tour first?'

'Actually, I had a sandwich at noon so I'm not really hungry. I hope you didn't wait for me?'

'No, as my mother always says, I'm a

178

growing boy. I ate around noon too. Maybe we could just have dessert later.'

'Maybe,' Amanda agreed. 'Why don't you give me the grand tour then?'

'Right this way.' He pulled a card from his shirt pocket and slid it in the slot. The door buzzed and popped open.

Amanda walked into a huge room and stopped dead in her tracks. The place was deserted. She whirled on him. 'Where is everyone?' she asked, accusingly.

'It's Friday. Everyone leaves at three on Friday.'

She looked at him suspiciously. 'But — ' she said, and stopped. Had he planned all along to get her alone?

'I'd wanted you to meet the gang, but you couldn't make it on time. Remember?' he asked gently.

Amanda felt like an idiot. The one thing she hadn't wanted was to be alone with him again. Now that had happened, and it was her own fault. She should just leave. She hesitated, indecisively gnawing her lower lip.

'Come on.' Harrison beckoned her. 'I've got something pretty exciting to show you.'

She sighed. She was a grown woman. Surely she could keep her hands — and her mouth — to herself. She'd just keep it light and impersonal.

'All right. But I can't stay long,' she said once again.

'This is where all functions other than design and production take place.' He gestured toward about two dozen cubicles with low walls dividing them. Computers, ten key calculators, and stacks of accounting ledgers lay on every work surface.

'I'd have never guessed.'

'Smart. Real smart,' he said. 'That's one reason I like you.'

'So you've decided I'm not just another pretty face,' she quipped, forcing a grin.

'Definitely not just a pretty face.' He led her to the door at the end of the room and opened it with his key card.

'These rooms along this hall are for

different projects we're working on.'

'I notice the doors all seem to be sound-proofed, and they all have those electronic locks on them.'

'Security is something you take very seriously in the computer industry. Even a stray word picked up by a delivery person might mean the difference in your getting a patent or your competitor getting it.'

'Is it really that cut-throat?'

'Never doubt it.' He opened one of the doors with his card.

'This is where we're working on that virtual reality project I mentioned.'

Amanda followed him into a room as large as her lab. Cables ran all over the place. An object that looked like a stereo headphone lay on a worktable.

Harrison pointed to it. 'Since I met you, and learned so much about the importance of smell, I've been wondering if we could include some kind of atomizer that would release a scent to coincide with the virtual reality script.'

'Wow. What an idea! You can do

that?' she asked, fascinated despite herself. She reached for the head-phones. 'How does this work?'

'Let me take your coat first.'

Amanda turned her back to him and shrugged out of the light wool garment.

Harrison draped it over his arm. He sniffed, liking the fragrance she wore.

'Sit here.' He wheeled a chair over for her, then reached for the headset and placed it over her ears. Strands of her silky hair brushed against his hands, making him lose his focus for a moment.

Amanda reached up and adjusted the earphones until they were comfortable. 'Okay. Now what.'

'Now, we swivel these tiny eyepieces down so they're lined up with your eyes.' He fiddled with them until he'd aligned them perfectly. 'Close your eyes. I'll start the program on the computer and tell you when to open your eyes.'

She heard him punching keys over on the computer keyboard. Then music filled the room. Or, she decided more accurately, it filled her ears. She grinned. She hadn't heard this kind of music since the last time she'd been at a carnival.

'Open your eyes, Amanda.'

She did and found herself on a carousel. 'Oh, this is wonderful.' She laughed along with the children around her and felt herself going up and down on the painted pony.

The experience was so real that she found it difficult to believe that she was sitting in a chair in a computer lab.

Suddenly it stopped. 'What happened?' she cried.

Harrison flipped the eyepieces out of the way. 'I stopped it. I wanted to ask you a question. What would be the perfect smell to go along with this?'

Amanda didn't need to think. 'Cotton candy.'

He nodded, grinning with delight. 'My thoughts exactly. Don't you think that would make the experience even more real to smell that spun sugar wafting through the air?'

'Yes,' she answered, her mind busy planning which ingredients would produce that wonderful aroma.

'What are you going to do with this when you get it perfected?'

'This project is for kids.'

Perplexed, she asked, 'Kids? I don't understand.'

'There's a lot of kids who are so sick they'll never see another carnival. Kids who suffer from birth defects or diseases that rob them of mobility. They'll never ride a carousel.

'I thought maybe this was a way they could experience something they can't do in the real world. Like go to a carnival. Ski down a mountain. Ride a horse. Dive off an Olympic platform. There's so many things they may never be able to do. Maybe they can have some of that fun through virtual reality.'

Something inside Amanda squeezed tight, making her heart feel as if it would burst. He really was different from any man she'd ever met. And that difference suddenly made his appearance meaningless.

'That's the nicest thing I've ever heard,' she said over the knot of emotion in her throat.

He shrugged. His bronzed cheeks flushed. He shrugged. 'I'm not so different from any other guy, but I'm glad you approve. Sometimes people don't get it. They wonder where the money is in a project like this.'

That was another reason he'd broken off his relationship with Marcy. She'd been openly disapproving of what she'd called his unrealistic altruism. Harrison removed the headset from Amanda and put it back on the worktable.

'But you're not doing this to get rich, are you?' she asked, softly. She used her fingers to fluff her hair.

He grinned. 'Nope. I'm doing it because it makes me feel good. I can just imagine some kid wearing this contraption — hopefully something smaller and sleeker — and laughing aloud like you did.'

He liked children too. Amanda wasn't even surprised. She hoped fiercely that he could get his virtual reality invention to the kids he'd intended it for.

'Come on. There's something else I want to show you.' He held out his hand.

Amanda stared at his hand. It seemed silly to with-hold her hand when she was on the verge of giving him her heart. Slowly, hesitantly, she placed her hand in his and looked into his eyes. The intensity there surprised her. Did he feel the connection between them that went far beyond a mere touch of hands? He squeezed her hand. She returned the slight pressure.

Maybe it had been inevitable from her first scent of him. Love at first smell. That would make an interesting story. She smiled at the thought.

'What do you want to show me now?' she asked, feeling rather emotional and uncertain about the threshold upon which she stood.

'Dessert!' He tucked her hand in the crook of his arm and led her out of the room.

Suddenly it no longer seemed a question of whether she should surrender to her feelings for Harrison. Rather, it was a question of did he feel an equal attraction to her. Did he want her to surrender to him?

'I don't know if I could eat anything,' she answered truthfully. She squeezed his arm, feeling the strength and the warmth of his body. He was no ninety-pound weakling.

This time their destination was the last office in the wing.

'Welcome to my world.' He opened the large door and ushered her into a spacious corner office. Windows on both sides flooded the room with light. She noticed that they were tinted, which probably kept the sunlight from being blinding, but didn't make it so dark that it looked dreary on an overcast day like today.

Harrison laid her coat on a burgundy

leather couch near the door. A slab of beveled glass on a chrome base occupied the space in front of the couch. An elegant chrome and walnut desk and a matching long credenza littered with electronic toys was in front of one window.

'Didn't your mother ever tell you to put your toys away when you finished with them?' Amanda asked, amazed at the many electronic gadgets lying about.

'Yeah, she did, but I wasn't a very neat kid.'

A square glass dining table and four chairs with Chinese red upholstery, which seemed a permanent fixture in the room, was set up in front of the other huge window.

Each of the giant windows offered a sweeping panorama of pine trees and gray sky that drew Amanda. She walked over to the window near the dining table.

'What a view!' Looking down, she saw a steady stream of traffic racing along the farm-to-market road that had once been two lanes and now boasted six and growing.

'Like it?' Harrison stood close behind her, invading her personal space.

With nervous, jerky movements, she put some space between them. 'Yes, it's a great view.' She looked at the table and saw goblets, white china, and silver flatware. Red roses filled the crystal bowl on the table and scented the air with their wonderful fragrance.

'Oh, my, you went to so much trouble,' she cried, feeling dismayed that she'd tried to stand him up.

'No trouble at all.' Harrison lifted a silver dome from a dish. 'Could I interest you in some quiche?'

'No, really. I couldn't eat a bite.' She knew she wouldn't be able to swallow over the lump in her throat.

'Not even some dessert?' He lifted another lid and revealed a two-inch thick wedge of cake that was so moist and dark Amanda could smell the Dutch chocolate used to make it. To her surprise, her mouth watered.

'Well, maybe just a bite.' Amanda sat on the chair he pulled out.

'I thought you'd appreciate this. Actually, my mother suggested it to me.'

'The roses?'

'No, I thought of the roses all by myself.' He grinned. 'I'm not quite as socially challenged as you may think.'

'No. I mean. I never thought you were.' Amanda blushed. She'd thought that and more, but suddenly none of that seemed to matter.

'What were you talking about then?' She leaned over closer to the table and saw delicate crystallized rose petals scattered around the cake slices.

'Oh, how lovely!'

'My mother suggested the chocolate cake, and she said to dress it up with these rose petals. You can get them at one of the caterers. They're real rose petals but they've been sugared. You can actually eat them.'

He picked one up and held it out to

her. Eyes fixed on him, she leaned closer and opened her mouth, taking the petal from his fingertips. She chewed slowly.

'What does it taste like?' he asked, softly.

'Delicious,' she lied. She couldn't have told him what it tasted like if her life had depended on it. All her thought processes were wrapped up in his eyes, his smell, his touch.

Harrison picked up one and placed it in his own mouth. He was so absorbed in watching her that he barely noticed the taste.

'You're right. It's exquisite.' *She* was exquisite. He wanted nothing more than to kiss her until she lost all her reservations about him.

With each hour that passed, the dishonesty of his charade tormented him. He wanted her to know him — the real him, not this stupid facade. He'd almost convinced himself that the only way out of this ridiculous situation was to make her as infatuated with him as he was with her. That way she wouldn't be so angry at his deception that she'd kick him out of her life.

'You're staring at me,' Amanda said.

'Sorry. I guess that must happen a lot?'

Amanda shrugged. 'I can't pretend that it doesn't. I've never known what the big deal was. To me, I don't look any different from anyone else. I mean, I'm just me. I see women who are more attractive than me all the time.'

He nodded. 'You're beautiful. You do know that, don't you?'

Amanda rolled her eyes. 'I've certainly heard it a lot, but, believe me, it's not all it's cracked up to be. Women are always jealous and men . . . ' She trailed off, not wanting to admit to him her miserable dating history.

'I guess men drive you nuts, always calling, always trying to seduce you.'

'Ha, if only you knew.' He could draw his own conclusion, she decided, feeling a bit guilty because she knew the conclusion he would reach was far different from the reality.

'How do you deal with it?'

'It's not hard,' she said flippantly. 'Smile, lead them on, toss them away when you're tired of them.'

His hands stilled. 'Is that how you femme fatales work?' He couldn't tell if she were being honest or just teasing.

'Sure. We've got more moves than a Mayflower van,' she quipped.

Surely she wasn't as shallow as she described. He couldn't have made such a mistake about her character. He watched her dig into the chocolate cake with enthusiasm. She savored every bite.

'Aren't you hungry?' she asked.

Oh, he was hungry, but chocolate cake and candied rose petals wouldn't sate his appetite. He made a noncommital reply and watched her enjoy the cake. The time had come for him to show this femme fatale some of his own moves.

Amanda patted her lips with the starched napkin. Relief swept through her. She'd toured the company, eaten dessert, and was moments away from a graceful getaway. Getting up and leaving now would be the easy way out. And maybe that was the best way for now, until she figured out what he wanted from their relationship.

'That was delicious.' With practiced nonchalance, she glanced at her watch. 'I hate to eat and run, but I really need to get going if I want to beat the traffic.'

'Not so fast.' He reached out and laid his hand over hers.

Her smile faltered.

'I need your help with something.' His thumb stroked a slow, lazy circle on the back of her hand.

'What's that?' she asked, not knowing if she wanted to hear the answer.

'Let's move over to the couch where we can get more comfortable, and we'll discuss it.' He stood and walked around to her side of the table.

Alarm bells went off in Amanda's head. She should run. She'd made her decision. But how could she discover what he wanted from their relationship if she kept running away? So much for the easy way out.

'I'm just fine where I am.'

'No, let's get away from this messy table. I'm sure the smell of all this food is affecting your nose.' He pulled her chair out with her in it.

'No, really it's not.' When he placed his hands on her shoulders, Amanda shot out of the chair. 'Well, maybe I would be more comfortable on the couch.' She couldn't seem to make herself leave, but she was too nervous to stay. What a quandary!

Amanda hurried over to the leather couch and chose the very middle, knowing he'd have to sit close to her. She perched on the edge, legs squeezed together to stop their trembling. Maybe she would discover what he wanted now.

Please, let it be me that he wants!

Harrison joined her on the couch, sitting at the far end, taking care not to brush against her.

'I think you and I should — ' He pursed his lips, unable to say what he really wanted to say for fear he would frighten her off. She seemed as jumpy as a wild deer.

'Should what?' Amanda asked. Her heart pounded. What if he said they should kiss? Or make love? What would she say? Stupid question! She shivered, imagining his touch, his kiss, his body against hers. She hoped she had enough decorum left not to immediately jump into his arms.

'Should what?' she prompted, breathless to hear his response.

'Are you sure you have time to do this?' he asked suddenly.

'Yes. Oh, yes.' She waited breathlessly to hear his proposal. Her eyes widened at that word and its implications. Suddenly all she wanted in the world were three little words.

I love you.

Followed by four more little words.

Will you marry me?

Amanda willed him to say them with every ounce of her being.

'Should what?' she asked again.

'Should discuss getting your uncle and my mother together.'

12

'Should what?' Amanda screeched. She stared at him. Surely he hadn't said what she thought. He was supposed to be whispering sweet nothings in her ear while he nibbled his way up her arm to her mouth. Where was the seductive proposition he was supposed to make? Where were the romantic declaration and the loving proposal?

Harrison leaned back and rested his arm on the back of the leather sofa.

'I was thinking after you mentioned your Uncle Leon that maybe he and my mother would hit it off. It sounds as if they're both lonely. Your uncle needs something more to fill his days than golf, and I know Mom needs something to keep her busy other than matchmaking.'

He was proud of himself. He'd managed to surprise Amanda completely. If he could just keep her off-balance enough to make his way into her life and heart, he'd be able to reveal his real self without risk of losing her.

Amanda stared at him. There really was something wrong with her! There had to be. Hang the proposal! At the moment, she'd have settled for a lusty proposition! Other women got propositioned all the time, but she never did.

'I thought maybe we could plan a dinner at my place Sunday night and get them together. I've already invited Mom to have dinner with you and me.'

'Don't you think you should have asked me first about Sunday night before inviting your mother?' she asked, wanting to lash out at him for something — anything.

'Of course, you're right. Are you doing anything Sunday night?' he asked, grinning. 'Before you answer, remember this is for the good of two people we both care about who don't deserve to be alone in life.'

'Put that way, I can't very well refuse.'

'Great! Shall we say six-thirty for an early dinner then?'

'Sure. Fine. Why not?'

'Great!' Harrison stood. 'Come on and I'll walk you down.'

'I'm leaving?' Amanda asked, feeling more bewildered by the moment. True, she wasn't very experienced, but she honestly didn't understand how she had misread him so completely.

'I know you have a lot of work to do,' he said, taking her arm and heading to the elevator. 'Right?'

'Right,' she mumbled. She was getting thoroughly irritated at his intense looks that promised so much, his husky-voiced innuendoes. And no follow-through! They'd shared one kiss — true it had been hot enough to melt glass — but when was he going to progress to something a little more stimulating? She just couldn't be that wrong about him.

At the elevator, she said stiffly, 'You don't have to see me down.' He sure seemed in a hurry to get rid of her.

'All right,' he said easily. 'I'm glad you came over, and I'm glad you understand about my virtual reality project.'

He might as well have been talking to a salesman, she thought, confused.

'No problem,' she snapped. She looked up at him and was surprised to see that smoldering look in his eyes again. She felt like screaming. What was his problem?

Suddenly, she realized that maybe he was shy. That would fit with her perception of geeks — shy and generally lacking social skills. So maybe he did want her but he didn't know how to act on it. Excited, she decided that maybe, just maybe, he was waiting for her to make the first move.

Amanda took a hesitant step toward him. He grinned at her and stuck his hand out for her to shake.

Irritated, she reached up, grabbed a handful of his hair, not even wincing as her fingers touched the wet mop, and pulled his head down to hers. His mouth opened in surprise. Amanda plastered her mouth to his and gave it everything she had.

Somewhere in the ensuing moments, he took her in his arms, holding her close. That wonderfully intoxicating musky scent of his swamped her and made her head reel. Her tongue touched his, thrust and parried in the age-old advance and retreat. He tasted wonderful! He felt wonderful!

Amanda felt his heart pounding against her breasts. Her heartbeat kept cadence with it. Every inch of her that touched him tingled in the most delightful way.

Her last coherent thought was that this kiss was even better than the first one they'd shared. Then she stopped thinking and only felt. Felt his mouth moving on hers, shaping her lips, devouring her, deepening the kiss. Felt his hands roving over her back, her sides, as if urgent to find purchase. Felt his body, which wasn't shy at all in its response to her and told her that she hadn't been wrong in thinking he wanted her.

When they'd used up every molecule of air in their lungs, they broke apart, gasping.

Amanda stared into his eyes.

The elevator bell dinged, and the door opened. Amanda stepped in. Without a backward glance, she stabbed the button for the ground floor. Mercifully, the door slid shut immediately and started down.

The mirrored walls of the elevator car reflected back her slightly dazed expression — and her smug smile. Though her knees shook, she couldn't help but feel a heady sense of satisfaction. That guy could kiss! But so could she.

Take that, Mr. Harrison Kincaid!

★   ★   ★

When Amanda stepped outside Harrison's building, her exultation faded. It was later than she thought, and evening was creeping into the gray day. The wind had picked up, and it was much colder. That's when she realized she'd forgotten her coat in his office.

She pulled out her key ring and punched the button to turn off the alarm and climbed into her Vette. No way would she go back to retrieve the coat. She'd rather freeze than spoil her grand exit by a hasty return.

She hoped he'd think about her all night — just as she'd spent every waking hour since their first meeting — thinking about him. Two could play this game of on-again, off-again attraction, or whatever the heck it was that Harrison was playing.

★   ★   ★

By late Saturday, Harrison decided that he'd discovered a new kind of hell, one not covered by biblical text. Either that or Amanda had set out to turn his brain to mush. Fried mush at that. At least that's what was going to happen if she kept running her fingers through his hair and jolting him with her own personal brand of electricity.

'Now isn't that much better?' she cooed. She smiled at his reflection in the salon's mirror.

Harrison couldn't say a word. He was concentrating on controlling his reaction to her touch. All he could think was how much he appreciated the stylist's cape that covered him from his neck to his knees.

'Wow!' Nicole said.

'Don't get any ideas,' Jim said, pulling Nicole closer to him.

'You clean up real good, Harrison.' Nicole grinned and pecked Jim on the cheek. 'But I'm spoken for. Right?'

'Right!' Jim kissed her back, on the lips.

Harrison wondered what Amanda would do if he suddenly grabbed her and did that. Better yet, what would she do if he swooped her into his arms and kissed her like she'd done him yesterday at the elevator?

If she'd given him any encouragement, he'd have been glad to try, because that woman could kiss. She'd certainly made him nearly melt into a puddle at her feet yesterday.

Today though, she'd been unusually quiet. At mid-morning, he'd met her, Nicole, and Jim at a men's clothing store, and he was thankful it was one he didn't usually patronize. He'd played along as Amanda and Nicole had matched ensembles, selected ties, and sent him to the dressing room.

He hadn't let her see him in the clothes he'd tried on. He thought it best to wait until the day of the wedding to reveal that he wasn't quite the geek she thought him to be. Yeah, he was still scared about what she'd do when she discovered his little subterfuge. With luck, she'd view it as a dumb joke. If he wasn't lucky, well, that didn't bear thinking about.

He'd decided that he would bind her to him before he revealed the truth. Since he was an old-fashioned kind of guy, he figured the best way to do that was through romance and great sex.

Judging by her kiss, he figured she expected that. What she wouldn't expect, though, was his declaration of love.

The idea was so new and so fragile that he could hardly think about it without getting the shakes. But somehow, he knew it was right. Maybe Mom was correct about her theory of the one person in the world who completed you and made you whole, he thought.

The foursome had laughed through the morning, but Amanda had seemed strangely preoccupied. He began to wonder if she'd been embarrassed by the incident at the elevator.

When they'd arrived at the hair salon, Amanda had come alive — flitting around, laughing too much, and touching him without seeming aware that it was making him crazy! He'd got to the point where he shied away from her tantalizing fingers. A man could only take so much.

At the moment, he felt like a lab specimen with all of them crowded around him, and the stylist sashaying back and forth as he snipped a final hair here and there.

'Well, that will have to do,' the stylist said, stepping back, crossing his arms, and admiring his handiwork.

'Raoul, you did a remarkable job,' Amanda exclaimed. 'Why, he looks like a different person.'

The stylist whipped the cape from him. 'That's because I'm the best, darling. You know that.'

Harrison nodded at his well-groomed reflection and got to his feet. He paid the bill while Amanda booked an appointment with Raoul for the morning of the wedding.

By evening, several hundreds of dollars poorer and sexually aroused beyond belief, Harrison sat next to the woman he loved in a restaurant booth opposite Nicole and Jim. The woman he loved! He suppressed the desire to sweep her into his arms right now and tell her.

'You've got to try this Hawaiian

chicken,' Nicole said, slicing off a chunk and laying it on Jim's plate.

Silently, Amanda watched her friend and Jim playfully exchange bites of food. She was so nervous that she could hardly hold her knife and fork.

'I like your new look,' Amanda said. She brushed a lock of his hair off his forehead. The strands were silky to the touch. He'd been just as irresistible with his hair slicked down, though.

'Thanks.' He squirmed and edged away from her.

Amanda found it difficult to keep her hands off him even though he seemed uncomfortable. She sighed. Somehow, she no longer noticed his looks.

With geeky hair and clothes, or with this new style and trendy clothes, he was still Harrison — a witty, charming, desirable man more interested in a child's joy than in making a fortune.

Unfortunately, he also seemed oblivious to her attempts to excite him. Since Harrison had bid her good morning, she'd done everything she could to make him aware of her. So far nothing seemed to be working. Why couldn't he see that she wanted him? Wanted him in the most elemental way a woman could want a man. She sighed. What was she going to have to do to get the message across to him?

'What's the matter? Isn't your grilled shrimp good?' Harrison asked.

'Oh, it's fine. I guess I'm just tired.' Amanda smiled at him and forked a bite of bacon-wrapped shrimp into her mouth. She chewed. It might as well have been rubber for all the pleasure she derived from it.

The conversation flowed around her as Jim and Harrison, prodded by Nicole, talked about computers. By the time their death-by-chocolate dessert was placed in front of them, she despaired of ever seducing Harrison.

'Guess we better get you to bed early tonight,' Harrison said. 'You look like you need about twelve hours of good, uninterrupted sleep.'

Somehow, this day of teasing him

and turning him on just wasn't working out the way she thought it would. Heart pounding, she decided to be as direct as she could.

'Well, we kind of thought we'd go dancing. Don't you want to come along?' Jim asked.

'No. Maybe next time,' Harrison said. He'd planned a different ending to their day of shopping, but Amanda did seem exhausted.

Just then she scooted closer to him and leaned her head on his shoulder.

He felt an immediate, nearly painful reaction. He put his arm around her shoulders, feeling a strange combination of protectiveness and excitement. Well, the excitement would just have to wait, he decided, suppressing the urge to lean down and place a kiss on her tousled blonde hair.

'Looks like it's time to call it a day,' he said. Amanda had closed her eyes.

He was as dense as the thick chocolate they were all eating! Amanda wanted to punch him. Couldn't he see that she wanted to be close? That she wanted to be held? She took a deep breath and told herself to do something. Anything.

'Well, we'll drop you off at your car, Harrison, then we'll take Amanda home.'

'Okay, that's — ' Harrison froze. His nerve endings leaped in excitement. Amanda's hand had slid onto his thigh. He opened and closed his mouth, but no words came out. All the blood in his brain rushed pell-mell to a different part of his anatomy.

'You all right, Harrison?' Jim asked

Harrison nodded. His throat was too dry to speak. Amanda shifted closer. Had she fallen asleep? Her hand moved up his thigh.

'You've got the strangest look on your face,' Jim said. 'Was the shrimp spoiled?'

Harrison shook his head. He couldn't have said a word if his life had depended on it. He looked closely at Amanda. Her dark lashes cast shadows against her cheek. Her eyes didn't move. She breathed deeply as if in a sound sleep.

Disappointed, he moved her hand back to her side. He just couldn't take the added stimulus. Even polyester had its stretchability limits.

'I think we'd better get Sleeping Beauty here to bed,' he said, his voice strained. He shook her gently to wake her.

Feeling completely rejected, Amanda opened her eyes and looked into his dark gaze. She'd tried everything she could think of to get him to respond, but he'd just seemed to grow more distant as the evening had progressed. She hoped he couldn't see how devastated she felt by his rejection.

Apparently, she needed a remedial flirting class or something. She just couldn't seem to get him aroused. Or worse, despite their kisses, he really didn't want her — that way.

That hurt more than Amanda had thought possible. Of course, she'd never felt this way about a man before. Harrison was the very first to excite her emotions as well as her body. It occurred that he'd make a great friend, but the thought depressed her. Maybe they could be friends *and* lovers.

If this is love, Amanda thought, *it stinks!*

13

'Call me an idiot,' Amanda said as she wheeled into the parking lot at Harrison's condo.

'Okay, you're an idiot,' came the voice from her cell phone.

'Gee, Nicole, you don't have to sound so cheerful about it.'

'If you think there's no future with Harrison, why are you having dinner with him and his mother tonight?'

Amanda cut the engine. 'I told you this is for my Uncle Leon and Lynn. I happen to agree with Harrison that the two of them are perfect for each other.'

She gathered her shoulder bag and stepped out of her car. 'Listen, I'll give you a full report later.' She pressed the button to end her call and dropped her phone into her purse.

The curving sidewalk leading to Harrison's front door was lit by fixtures discreetly hidden beneath mounds of monkey grass.

Amanda took a deep breath and pressed the doorbell. Harrison opened the door before the sound of the chime faded. He took her breath away. She hadn't seen him in anything but the polyester. Tonight he was in camel tan pleated wool slacks and an ivory long-sleeved designer knit shirt. His hair was full, soft, and appeared very touchable. At least, her fingers itched to touch the dark strands.

He looked so good it was all she could do not to stare. The one thing that hadn't changed was his scent. It was the same intoxicating smell that had initially attracted her.

'Mom's here already,' he cautioned in a whisper. 'Turning the tables is going to be fun.'

His good humor was infectious. Amanda relaxed. If all he wanted was friendship, then that's all she would offer him, she decided, wistfully.

'Uncle Leon should be here in a few

minutes. Does your mother suspect anything?'

'No, I told her you were bringing over your uncle because he wanted to check me out.'

'Quick thinking. I told Uncle Leon that you wanted to discuss the possibilities of a joint venture with Scent From Heaven. He thinks you want me to work on adding an odor device to your virtual reality project.'

'Now that's not just quick thinking, that's psychic. I really would like you to work on that with me.'

'Really?' Amanda felt an excitement that had a poignant edge to it. She didn't think she could manage to be around him all the time — wanting him as much as she did. Love was hell!

'Really. I can see all kinds of possibilities for adding smell to experiences.'

So could she, but none she could discuss in front of his mother, who had suddenly appeared in the foyer.

'Aren't you going to bring your guest

in, Harrison?' Lynn Kincaid asked.

'Sure. We just started talking business, and I forgot my manners.'

A few minutes later, Amanda settled into the deep cushions of the chamois-colored couch in the living room. The room was comfortably worn but rather plain. An oversized poster of the basketball Dream Team from a few years back occupied the space over the fireplace. The expensively framed poster, which appeared to be signed by the players, was nice but certainly nothing she'd have hung in such a prominent place.

'It does lack a woman's touch, doesn't it?' Lynn asked, watching Amanda.

'Oh, no. It's very nice.'

Lynn chuckled. 'That's okay, dear. I agree with you. I'm sure you could do wonders with it.'

Amanda laughed nervously. 'That's not what our relationship is about. We're just friends. I really have to thank you for coercing your son into escorting me to my cousin's wedding.'

Lynn studied her for a long moment.

Hadn't Amanda and Harrison fallen for each other yet? When she'd seen them whispering together, she'd been certain they had. The air around them fairly zinged with electricity. Now she wasn't so sure.

She allowed Amanda to change the subject, and soon they were chatting as if they'd known each other forever. They were discussing department store perfumes when the doorbell rang.

'Are you expecting anyone else?' Lynn asked.

'Oh, it's just my Uncle Leon,' Amanda answered. 'I asked him to join us this evening. I might be working on Harrison's virtual reality project. Excuse me a moment.' She went to the door with Harrison.

Alone in the room, Lynn frowned and threw up her hands in disgust. 'Working together? I don't believe it! I'm beginning to think young people today don't know beans about sex!'

A moment later Amanda and Harrison brought the new guest to the living room. Lynn looked up. Her eyes widened in surprise. Amanda's Uncle Leon was lean and athletic looking. His rugged face attested to years of disregarding admonitions to avoid sunshine. He was tanned and healthy looking.

Unlike her late husband, he had very little hair left, but he could easily be placed in that Sean Connery category of older, balding men — still sexy and attractive despite the years. In other words, as they said nowadays, Leon Whitfield was a hunk. A mature hunk.

Lynn took a deep breath and tried to make some sort of civil response to the introductions.

'Dinner's ready,' Harrison said, shepherding them to his small dining room. He'd arranged two chairs on either side of the rectangular table, and he seated Leon and Lynn together on the same side.

'Amanda, would you help me in the kitchen?'

'Sure. What can I do?' She followed

him through the bifold louvered doors. When she got on the other side, she closed the doors, leaving a narrow crack through which she peered.

'What are they doing?' Harrison whispered close to her ear.

'They're talking.' She could hardly breathe with him so close.

'I think this was brilliant, if I do say so myself.'

When she felt him move away, she turned. 'What can I do to help?'

'Can you dress the salad and toss it? It's in the fridge. The dressing is in a jar in the door rack.'

She did as he directed, pouring the vinaigrette over the mixed greens, chopped tomatoes, and black olives and tossing it thoroughly.

'What smells so spicy?' she asked, blinking rapidly.

'My specialty. I call it Cajun spaghetti.'

'Well, it smells good, but it makes my eyes burn just from the fumes. I'm almost afraid to ask what it contains.'

'The usual Italian ingredients — maybe a smidgen more of garlic. And the secret ingredient — a huge spoonful of cayenne pepper.'

Amanda stopped tossing. 'Oh, dear. I should have told you. Uncle Leon can't eat spicy foods.'

'That's all right, Mom can't either.' He grinned.

She looked at him in shock then burst into laughter. 'Why, that's downright Machiavellian!'

'Yeah. Pretty clever, huh? Now let's wait another ten minutes to be sure they're hooked on each other. The way they're talking together, that should be all it will take.'

They talked in low voices about the virtual reality project while Harrison sliced the loaf of crusty Italian bread hot from the bread machine on the counter.

By the time Amanda carried the salad to the table and Harrison followed her with the bread and a crock of warm butter, Leon and Lynn were engrossed in a discussion about the merits of a metal driver as opposed to a wood driver.

'Mom hates golf,' Harrison whispered to Amanda as he pulled out her chair.

'They can't take their eyes off each other,' she replied, excited for the two older people.

Throughout the salad course, any comments from Harrison and Amanda elicited only simple replies from Lynn and Leon. The two seemed not to be hungry since they hardly touched the salad and bread. Instead, they spent all their time talking to each other and laughing together.

When Harrison and Amanda brought in the huge bowl of pasta and spaghetti sauce, their two relatives were discussing the golden days of rock and roll.

'I just adored the Big Bopper,' Lynn said. 'For years, I would only wear Chantilly Lace perfume because of that song.'

Leon laughed. 'Actually, I've always thought that was one of the nicest fragrances a woman could wear.' He leaned closer to Lynn. His voice dropped low, but Amanda and Harrison, ears straining, heard him clearly say, 'I'm sure it smells wonderful on you, Lynn.'

Then, to Harrison's amazement, his mother blushed like a schoolgirl and said, 'That could be arranged.' He glanced at his watch. It was time to move things along.

'We'd better serve ourselves. The spaghetti is getting cold, though the hot sauce will still warm you up.'

'Oh, Harrison, no! You didn't put any of that red fire in there, did you?' Lynn asked.

Harrison struck his forehead with the heel of his hand. 'What was I thinking? Mom, I'm sorry. I clean forgot.'

'What's the problem?' Leon asked, frowning.

'This is what Harrison thinks is his trademark dish. It has a ton of cayenne pepper in it. It smells wonderful and tastes equally good, but every time I eat it, I get sick. I just can't take that cayenne anymore,' Lynn explained.

'Hmmm. Neither can I,' Leon said.

'Oh, dear, and I'm just starving,' Lynn said plaintively. 'I bet you don't have anything else in the house knowing you.'

Harrison shrugged. 'Sorry, Mom. I really goofed. I can order a pizza, if you like.'

She shuddered. 'No, thank you, dear. I'll just wait until I go home and have a snack.'

'Oh, no. We can't have that,' Leon said. 'Actually, I'm ravenous too, Lynn. I have a solution, Harrison, though it's a little unorthodox. Why don't your mother and I go have some dinner? I mean, it's been fun visiting with you and Amanda, but Lynn and I need something to eat. You know how it is when you get older and are used to regular meals.'

'But, Uncle Leon, you hardly ever eat regular meals.' Amanda exclaimed in honest amazement.

Leon laughed. 'You're wrong, Amanda. I'm really set in my habits.'

'And I am too,' Lynn hastily said. 'I just hate it when my blood sugar drops because of too much time between meals.'

'Yes, me too, Lynn. Me too!' Leon exclaimed.

'We'll just say good night for now, Amanda. It was lovely seeing you again. We can all have dinner another night. You don't mind terribly, do you, Harrison?'

'No, that's fine, Mom. If that's what you want to do.'

Leon nearly jumped out of his chair and held Lynn's chair as she rose quickly.

'This has been lovely,' Lynn said. 'Just let me know when you'd like to do it again.'

'What about discussing business?' Harrison asked as he and Amanda followed them to the foyer.

'Oh, we'll get to it,' Leon promised. 'Next time.'

Lynn opened the coat closet and found her suede jacket.

'Here, let me help you with that,' Leon said, taking the coat from her and holding it.

He seemed as eager as a schoolboy on his first date, Amanda thought, and the way Lynn giggled and blushed, anyone would have thought she was on a first date too. She remembered what Harrison had said and realized that in a sense, Lynn was on a first date. Gosh, she hoped this worked out. It had certainly started off like gangbusters.

Lynn giggled. 'Thank you, Leon,' she purred.

Leon kissed Amanda on the cheek and tweaked her nose. 'I often forget how clever you are, but you always remind me in the most delightful ways.'

Amanda smiled. 'Enjoy your dinner, Uncle Leon.'

They hurried out as if every minute counted. And maybe it did, Amanda thought. Maybe they knew it wasn't wise to waste time. Was that a lesson she should take to heart?

Harrison closed the door and leaned against it. 'I'm starved. How about you?'

'I could eat something.'

'I have some nice sliced roast from the deli and a robust chianti waiting for us.'

A tap on the door interrupted him. He opened it.

Lynn stepped in. 'I forgot my purse.' She hurried to the living room and returned with it.

'Not bad for an amateur,' she said, kissing her son on the cheek. 'Not bad at all!'

Then she hurried out, closing the door behind her.

Harrison and Amanda looked at each other and burst into laughter. They laughed so hard they had to hang on to each other to remain upright.

Finally, he wiped his eyes and said, 'Come on. Let's get a glass of that chianti. This definitely calls for a celebration.'

Despite her reservations, Amanda

soon found herself sitting on one of the stools at the kitchen counter while Harrison poured the dark red wine.

He lifted his glass. 'To matchmaking.'

'Hear, hear!' She clinked her glass against his.

Harrison watched her sip the wine. She was more relaxed today than yesterday and seemed to be enjoying the evening. He wondered how he could maneuver her out of the kitchen and to a more intimate setting.

Silence fell between them. After a few minutes of sipping her wine, Amanda said, 'I really should be leaving soon.' She didn't want to leave, but Harrison seemed so preoccupied that she didn't know whether she should stay.

She glanced at her watch. 'I might be able to get some work done tonight.'

'Work?' He repeated. All of his hopes for the evening ahead crumbled. He didn't want her to go. He wanted her to stay with him — all night. For the first time in his life, he was at a loss as to how to communicate that to a woman he fancied. With other women, there'd never been this much at stake. He searched for an excuse to keep her here.

Amanda waited, hoping he would entreat her to stay. She looked around the room, her eyes jumping from the stove to the sink, to the computer. Computer? She laughed. 'I can't believe you have a computer in the kitchen.'

'Why not? I spend a lot of time in here.' He grinned sheepishly. 'Actually, I like to cook. I find it relaxing after a long day of dealing with binary code and microchips to handle such commonplace ingredients as tomatoes and peppers.'

'At the end of the day, potato chips have more appeal than microchips?'

'Something like that,' he agreed. He seized this as the perfect excuse to prolong her visit. He stood and walked over to the computer and powered it up.

'I can go on the Internet and find recipes with step by step instructions when I want to try something new.'

She carried her stool over to the end

of the counter where the computer sat. Harrison followed. He stood behind her. He was so close, she could feel his breath against her cheek when he leaned over her to click the icon for his Internet service.

'You really need a website,' he said. 'Scent From Heaven could go global in days.'

'I'm content creating perfumes for the rich and famous, or infamous, of Houston.'

'But you could sell internationally with very little effort.'

'You're right. I could create a fragrance to market to one and all, but the competition for something like that is fiercer than you think.'

'It seems like there's a new designer fragrance every time I walk through a department store.'

Amanda nodded. 'Unfortunately, that's too true. In the last decade, more than eight hundred new brands were introduced, but demand didn't increase along with that.'

'I didn't know that.'

Amanda shrugged. 'Lifestyles have changed. And there's more recognition of allergies so people don't use scent the way they once did. To make a long story short, perfume sales have dropped.'

Amanda drank some wine. 'I'm not saying the perfume business is at risk. It'll never die. It's just that it isn't as easy to go global as you may think.'

Harrison leaned over to type in a web address. Amanda watched a site open and a page begin to download, appearing bit by bit on the monitor. She couldn't have said what the site was. Her focus was on the musky scent rising from Harrison.

'Does your computer at the lab have a graphical interface?' he asked, still leaning over her. Now his chest pressed into her shoulder. Amanda didn't think she could stand it if he didn't move. Yet if he moved away, she'd go berserk. Either way, she was in a quandary.

'Interface?' Her voice quavered. She cleared her throat. 'What's an interface?'

She turned and looked up at him. He was so close that she could see the different striated markings in the dark irises of his eyes. To her surprise, there was amber and a bit of green.

Her eyes dropped to his lips. She felt dizzy with the desire to close the distance between his mouth and hers.

'Interface,' he said. As she watched, his pupils dilated until they were enormous in his eyes. He cleared his throat. 'An interface is the surface forming a common boundary of two spaces or bodies.'

'Two bodies?'

'Yes. Where . . . where independent systems communicate with each other,' he stammered.

'Like we're communicating with each other?' Amanda whispered, staring into his eyes.

'Exactly.' His voice was low and husky, a caress to her ears.

Her breath came in short gasps. 'Are we talking about computers?'

'Not anymore.' Harrison placed his

index finger under her chin and tipped her head up.

'It's awfully warm in here.' Amanda cradled her flushed cheeks with both palms.

He removed her hands from her face and placed them around his neck. His skin was as hot as hers. She closed her eyes as he closed the gap between their lips. That's when the sensual fireworks exploded. His groan excited her all the more.

Frantically her hands tugged at his shirt, wanting to touch his skin — desperate to touch his skin. He obliged her and jerked his shirt off and tossed it away.

'Oh! You are beautiful!' she whispered, awestruck at the curling dark hair that covered his chest and arrowed down below his belt. She pressed her face to his chest and kissed the flat nipples.

Harrison thought his legs would collapse. Her hands ran over his body, stroking, delineating the muscles, and driving him half insane.

'Amanda,' he whispered, reverently touching her shoulders, sliding his hands into her blonde mane. He held her head away from his chest so he could kiss her even more passionately.

His hands moved down her throat, over her shoulders, and onto her breasts. Amanda sucked in a startled breath. She had no idea his touch could make her feel like this — desperate, needy, hungry for more.

His fingers went to the buttons of her shirt. He hesitated. His eyes silently asked and she answered, 'Yes, please, touch me.'

But his fingers shook so hard that he couldn't work the small buttons. Smiling and feeling a heady sense of power at her hold on him, Amanda loosened the buttons. He slid the shirt from her shoulders, and it fell at their feet.

'You're beautiful,' he said, fingers tracing the dark nipples barely hidden by the lacy cups.

Amanda wasted no time in unclasping the bra and tossing it behind her. She felt no shyness, nor did she feel brazen either. She felt only a sense of rightness about this.

'You're blushing,' he said, lowering his head to kiss her perfect breasts.

'Oh! I had no idea!' she whispered, pressing his head closer. 'I'm going to melt if you don't stop,' she said.

'Promise?'

'Oh, yes! Definitely.'

His head raised a fraction of an inch. 'It's much cooler in my bedroom.'

'Wonderful.' She raised herself on tiptoe and encircled his neck with her arms, locking her hands together. Her body sagged against his.

'You're trembling,' he marveled.

'It's all that talk about interfaces and computers. It makes me so excited I can hardly stand it. Do you think there's a common boundary between our two bodies?'

'I suggest we do a little research and find out.' His mouth covered hers.

Amanda moaned. Why had they waited so long to do this? Surely it had been centuries since she'd fallen in love with him. The kiss went on and on, drugging her senses and hinting at the passion seething inside him.

When he lifted her into his arms, Amanda didn't protest. In fact, if she could have, she'd have purred in pure satisfaction because she was exactly where she'd wanted to be for days.

14

Harrison took his time. He seemed to know just where to touch her to make her shiver in response. He knew when to stroke her gently and when to exert more pressure. He knew exactly the moment when she needed him to fill her, and he complied in a way that robbed her body of strength and breath, yet renewed her at the same time.

Though Amanda wasn't as sexually experienced as most women her age, she knew instinctively that Harrison was the kind of lover women always hoped to find, but seldom did.

Her heart thundered and her body arched against his. Amanda trembled, physically and emotionally, as she came ever closer to climax.

Harrison wanted to tell her he loved her, but he felt dishonest when he hadn't told her the truth yet about his charade. He gritted his teeth as he tried to restrain his own release as well as the words that reverberated in his mind.

Primitive male instinct took over and he lost one part of his battle when Amanda stiffened in his arms and cried out. Suddenly, he couldn't control himself. That had never happened before. He thrust into her again and again until he was spent.

Exhausted and dripping with sweat, he collapsed over her. After a few moments when he discovered he was still alive, he nuzzled her neck and lavished her with meaningless compliments.

Amanda lay silent. So this was what lovemaking was like, she thought, feeling rather dazed. She'd almost confessed her love for him. Surely, that was what he was really trying to communicate to her, wasn't it?

Her hands moved restlessly over him as if seeking something, perhaps the truth, from his beautifully muscled body. She'd been surprised to see he was tanned everywhere except an area that must be covered by a brief pair of boxer-style swim trunks in the summer. Nothing about him fit her picture of a geek.

A small part of her brain wondered if all geeks were this fantastic in bed.

'What are you thinking about?' he asked, propping up on his left elbow.

'I was just wondering if all, uh, computer experts, were this good in bed.'

'Were you now?' His right hand splayed across her breast. He squeezed gently.

To Amanda's chagrin, her body responded, heating immediately. She now knew that Harrison had the power to soothe the restless hunger that besieged her.

'Computers aren't nearly this much fun,' Harrison said, his mouth lowering to hover above one nipple. 'I could never design something this beautiful.'

Her hands tangled in his hair as she pressed him to her breast. His scent was wonderful, Amanda thought. Her pheromone receptors must be working overtime, just as his production of pheromones was. That was the last coherent thought she had.

The first time they had made love, it had been fast and frantic as if they chased something that might escape if they didn't move quickly enough. But this time, it was deliciously slow and languid as they learned the pleasures of each other's bodies.

They spent the better part of the next few hours trying — and succeeding — to drive each other wild with desire. Finally, sated and too tired to do much beside sleep, they still lay awake, occasionally stroking, talking drowsily.

'I think I owe this cousin of yours a thank-you note,' Harrison said.

Amanda giggled. 'Why would you say that?'

'Well, if she hadn't been getting married, you wouldn't have needed a date for her wedding. So we would never have met.'

'I guess that's true,' Amanda said.

'It's only proper' — he kissed her

hand — 'that I thank what's-her-name.' He sucked the tip of her pinky finger into his mouth and teased it with his tongue.

'Marcy,' Amanda breathed, marveling that just a fingertip could have so many nerve endings. 'Marcy Barnwell.'

Harrison froze. In fact, he felt as if the blood suddenly froze in his veins. 'What did you say?'

'My cousin is Marcy Barnwell. She's a lawyer with a firm downtown.'

Harrison felt his heart turn over. What were the odds that there were two women lawyers in Houston with that name?

'Yes, dear Cousin Marcy,' Amanda said, affecting a British accent. 'Studied at Oxford where she picked up this veddy veddy British way of talking.'

That cinched it. That was the Marcy he'd dated last year. When he'd broken it off, he hadn't chosen the best occasion to do it. Unfortunately, Marcy had decided they needed to become intimate and was trying to get him in the sack. To say she'd been bitter and vindictive was an understatement. Despite her upper class affectations, the woman had a sewer of a mouth, he'd discovered that day.

Amanda's voice lapsed into her normal soft Texas drawl. 'She's been the bane of my existence ever since I can remember.'

'Why is that?' he asked cautiously. His mind raced furiously as he tried to figure out what to do. Should he tell her? Should he remain silent? But then Marcy would reveal it at the wedding — unless he could hide in the crowd. Amanda had said there'd be hundreds of guests. Dare he take the chance she wouldn't find out? Next to this, his charade became even more threatening. What a fool he'd been!

'Hardly. The only reason I'm going to her wedding is because of family pressure.' Then, bit by bit, she told Harrison about Marcy's insults, revealing far more about herself than she thought.

Harrison leaned over her, wishing he

could have been there when Amanda had her senior prom. He'd have taken her. He'd have showered her with corny Valentines and gooey candy. He'd been so wrong about her. Feeling her wonderful body snuggled in his arms, it was difficult to believe that she'd never had a serious boyfriend. Suddenly, he was fiercely glad that she hadn't. If she'd been as popular as her arrogant cousin, she wouldn't have been available when he'd finally found her.

'Let's not talk about Marcy any-more,' Amanda suggested. 'I associate her name with a lot of hurt, and I don't want to spoil this time with you. Tonight is special. I want to remember it always.'

She rolled on top of him. 'Care to go for the best two out of three?' she asked softly.

★　★　★

At ten o'clock Monday morning, Amanda waltzed into the boutique.

244

'Good morning, Sherry!' she called, beaming at her sales associate.

'You sure seem in a good mood,' Sherry said.

'I'm in the best mood of my life. Oh, Sherry! I want to shout it from the rooftops!'

Nicole walked into the showroom from the back. 'Shout what?'

Amanda spread her arms wide as if to embrace the whole world! 'I'm in love. I'm in love! With the most wonderful man in the whole world!' She whirled around and around.

Nicole squealed and grabbed her to hold her still. 'Tell me. Tell me. With the geek?'

'Yes. With the geek! Isn't it grand?'

'Congratulations,' Sherry said. 'By the way, your dad and your mom each called this morning. They asked you to call them back as soon as possible.'

'Okey-doke,' Amanda chirped.

'Come into my office as soon as you finish returning your calls,' Nicole said.

Amanda floated to the lab. She was

certain that her feet didn't even touch down. Though she'd had only a few hours of sleep, she felt as energized as that little pink mechanical bunny on television.

Harrison had awakened her at dawn, in a way that made her shiver as she remembered. Then he'd pulled her into the shower with him and created another memory she'd treasure.

Fortified by coffee and toast and the sweetest goodbye kiss, she'd gone home to dress for the day. She stared at the phone, willing it to ring. Even though he was picking her up for lunch, she wanted to hear his voice.

As if in response to her willpower, the phone suddenly rang. Amanda grabbed it before it stopped. She tried not to sound disappointed when she heard her father's voice.

'Honey, I found that article about your boyfriend.'

'Oh, good. I'd love to see it.' *He isn't just my boyfriend*, her heart sang.

'Thing I don't understand is why you

thought he didn't care anything about clothes and stuff. It says here he was voted one of the ten best dressed men in Houston last year.'

A muffled conversation came through the phone. She heard her dad say, 'In a minute, Susie. Let me talk first.'

Amanda frowned. 'Would you repeat that, Dad?' When he said it a second time, her heart quit singing its happy tune. 'But, I don't understand.'

'Understand what, baby? There's a picture of him all decked out in some Italian suit. He looks pretty spiffy to me, but I guess you know more about fashions and trends than I do.'

'All right. All right, Susie,' Leland said. 'Baby, your mother's about to have a cow over something. I'm handing the phone to her and heading to the golf course.'

'Amanda? Amanda, are you all right?' Susie asked.

Was she all right? She didn't know. Five minutes ago, she'd never been better, but now? Something strange was going on. 'Sure, Mom. I'm okay.'

'I tried to call you several times last night, dear, to tell you this, but you didn't seem to be home.'

Amanda blushed hotly. 'Yes, well, I was, uh, busy.'

'I see,' Susie said, drawing out the two short words. She sighed deeply.

Amanda realized that her mother knew exactly what she'd been busy doing.

'I wish I had talked to you sooner, but I had to be sure.'

'Sure about what, Mom?' Suddenly, her hands shook. She had a feeling of impending doom. She sat on the desk to steady herself.

'I talked to Gwen the other day, and I was right. I had heard the name of Harrison Kincaid before. He and Marcy had a — that is, he and Marcy dated last year. Gwen really thought something serious might develop out of it, but then they suddenly broke up.'

'Thank you for calling, Mom,' Amanda said woodenly. 'I have to go now. Good-bye.' she hung up the phone even though her mother was still speaking.

Amanda sat without moving. She didn't know how long she'd been sitting there, staring blankly into space when Nicole came in. 'Hey, I thought you were going to come tell me about you and the geek?'

'He isn't a geek.'

'He isn't?' Nicole frowned. 'Say, are you all right?'

'And he isn't in love with me.'

'What do you mean?'

'I mean that I must be the biggest fool in the world.' Amanda told Nicole everything and felt a righteous indignation growing with each word she spoke.

'I agree. Hanging would be too good for the slime!' Nicole sat next to Amanda. 'But I don't understand why he would pretend to be this geeky guy.'

Amanda shrugged. 'I guess I'll never know, because I don't intend to see him again.'

'Maybe he thought because I was a

blind date that he'd have some fun with me! And maybe he thought I was so desperate I would be easy pickings.' She choked. Tears filled her eyes. 'And he was right.'

Nicole held her while she cried. 'There. There. He's not worth one single tear.'

'And then when I think he and Marcy were l-lovers — ' Amanda broke off, hating the thought of her cousin enjoying his kisses and caresses.

'There's no way he could have known you and Marcy were related. I don't think we ever mentioned her name. You only referred to her as 'my darling cousin.' Not that I'm defending the skunk. Harrison needs to be on the receiving end of a dirty trick. Wonder how he'd like it?'

Amanda hiccoughed. 'I wonder too.' Her breathing calmed and she turned a speculative gaze on Nicole.

'I think you're absolutely right.'

'I am? About what?'

'And I know just the trick to play.'

'Amanda, I don't like that look in your eye.'

'Leave me be, Nicole. I've got a cologne to mix before he arrives for lunch.'

'Oh, dear. You're not going to poison him, are you? I mean, I know what he did was sneaky and underhanded and dishonest, but maybe he has a good excuse.'

'Whose side are you on?' She shooed Nicole away. 'Don't worry. I'm not going to poison him. Now go.'

Amanda slipped into her coat and opened the cabinet beneath the sink. Good, she had a half bottle of pine oil. She walked out to the showroom and got her biggest atomizer bottle and a gift bag. When she was finished filling the bottle with disinfectant, she typed up a list of instructions and placed it in the bag with the flask. Then she took her business card and wrote on the back, slipped it into an envelope, wrote 'open last' on it before sealing it. She dropped that in the bag too.

★ ★ ★

A very troubled Harrison, who'd tossed his geeky clothes and worn his best suit, walked into Scent From Heaven precisely at noon. He'd decided to confess. He patted his suit pocket, taking courage from the three-carat diamond solitaire he'd purchased this morning. Surely Amanda would forgive him for the charade and for Marcy when she saw the engagement ring. At least he prayed she would.

To his dismay, Amanda wasn't there. The young woman at the counter said she'd been called away on urgent business but had left him a gift with instructions to open it as soon as he got home that evening.

Harrison took the gift bag and left. The first thing he did when he got back to the office was call her. After trying four more times, he gave up. She'd call him when she returned. By the time he went home, he was going nuts because she still hadn't called.

He took the gift bag to the bedroom and sat on the bed to open it. He smiled with pleasure. She'd created a cologne just for him! But it wasn't just any cologne. This one had a secret aphrodisiac as one of the ingredients. His smile widened as he read on.

Amanda planned to arrive at his place at precisely seven. Exactly five minutes before seven, he was to turn back the covers on the bed and undress. Then he was to soak the sheets and pillows with the special cologne and spray his body too, being certain to avoid his eyes and face. If he did this, she promised in her note, he'd have a night he'd never forget!

Harrison hurriedly shed his clothes. He only had a few minutes before she got here. He didn't think they needed any extra stimulus, but he bowed to Amanda's greater knowledge of scents. He turned down the covers and fluffed the pillows. Then he got the atomizer and started spraying. He was so enthusiastic about following her instructions that it wasn't until he'd sprayed his legs and arms that he realized what he was smelling didn't turn him on. He sniffed. It was horrible! His whole bed stunk!

Suspicious now, he stalked to the bathroom. He poured some of the special cologne in the toilet bowl and watched the water turn white.

'Amanda!' he roared. The smell seemed to be stuck inside his nose. He smelled like a bottle of pine oil.

Harrison didn't know what to do first. Strip the bed, burn the pillows, jump into the shower, or drive over to Amanda's and give her a piece of his mind!

In the end, he settled for the shower.

★   ★   ★

'Oh, baby, you look so beautiful,' Leland Whitfield said, pulling Amanda into his arms as she walked up the church steps. 'Are you my funny little Valentine?' he asked, as he'd done every Valentine's Day she could remember.

Amanda smiled weakly, feeling as pale as the fluffy white clouds overhead.

'That pink silk is utterly beautiful. I'm so glad your friends came with you today,' Susie said. 'Nicole, it's good to see you again. And, Jim, it's nice to meet you.'

Amanda listened to the conversation that flowed around her with half an ear. Jim was a painful reminder of Harrison. Her heart ached just thinking about him. She had refused to talk with him when he'd called, outraged over the pine oil prank. He hadn't called since. She'd stayed away from the lab, but he hadn't tried to see her there either, to her dismay.

'Shall we go in?' Amanda asked, feeling cold despite the sunny day.

'Oh, just another minute or two, dear,' Susie said. She looked behind Amanda and brightened. 'Oh, yes. Now we can go. Hurry along, Jim and Nicole. You too, Leland.' She grabbed her husband's arm and hustled the other couple ahead of her. What was her hurry? Amanda wondered, turning to look over her shoulder.

Harrison leaped up the last few steps. Amanda's heart did a somersault.

'What are you doing here?' she asked, trying not to feel joy at seeing him.

'I promised to escort you to this wedding, remember?'

'You're relieved of that promise,' she hissed.

He took her arm, but she tried to jerk it from his grasp. He held on firmly. 'I don't want to be relieved from it.'

Amanda and he engaged in a silent tug of war where her arm was the prize. When she began receiving odd glances from the other guests as they arrived, she ceased her ineffective struggle.

'What's the matter? Was that beautiful orange and blue suit in the cleaners today?' she asked nastily.

'Yeah, it stinks of pine oil.'

Amanda had the grace to blush and look guilty. 'Good. Then it must have obscured your skunk odor.'

'Come on folks, you need to get

inside the church,' one of the ushers said from the doorway.

'Shall we?' Harrison asked. 'I'm not letting go of your arm. You'd probably slam the church door in my face.'

Amanda stormed up the steps with him holding on to her. Once inside the church, they were ushered to the bride's side. Nicole's eyes widened when she saw Harrison. She moved closer to Jim, and Amanda, followed closely by Harrison, sat down.

Harrison had feared she wouldn't welcome him, but at least he had Susie and Leland on his side after he'd explained things. The rest was up to him.

When the wedding march started, everyone stood. He took that opportunity to watch Amanda. She looked extraordinarily beautiful in a sleek pink dress that made her skin glow. Her hair had been arranged on top of her head in some fancy style that made him want to remove the hairpins and watch it tumble down.

'You're supposed to be looking at the bride,' Amanda hissed. 'Her name is Marcy, in case you've forgotten.'

'I've seen her,' he replied. 'She can't hold a candle to you.'

She was a fool to listen to him, Amanda thought. But the other part, the silly romantic part of her brain, basked in his comment.

When they sat again and the ceremony began, Harrison prayed that he'd find a way to make Amanda believe that he loved her.

After what seemed like an eternity to both of them, trumpets blared, white doves were released, and the recessional was played. The guests followed the bride out. Harrison stepped out into the aisle to allow Amanda to pass. She took advantage of the chance to try to elude him.

'What are you? In training for the marathon?' he asked grabbing her arm halfway up the long aisle.

'You did your duty. You escorted me here,' she snapped. 'Now just go away.'

258

'Not until you listen to what I have to say.'

Her parents and Jim and Nicole caught up with them. 'Okay, Harrison and Amanda can ride with us,' Leland declared. 'That way we can get better acquainted.'

She was doomed, Amanda realized. The drive to the banquet room at the downtown hotel was conducted in dead silence. It was as if no one knew what to say. They took their place in the long line and waited to congratulate the groom and wish the bride best of luck.

As they inched up, Amanda felt Harrison's presence behind her. Thankfully, his charismatic scent was masked by all the other perfumes in the room. Yet, she still was all too aware of his nearness. Her traitorous body clamored for his touch.

'I never meant to hurt you, Amanda,' he whispered next to her ear, stirring the tendrils of hair that had escaped the crown of curls.

'Then why did you?' She hadn't

meant to answer him. It had just slipped out.

'It started innocently enough. I really didn't want to go on a blind date with you, but Mom had promised you.'

'Thanks, that makes me feel so much better,' she whispered, feeling bitter tears burn her eyes.

'I figured if you rejected me that I'd be off the hook.'

'So you dressed like a total and complete geek so I would reject you?'

'Stupid but true. Then I took one look at you.'

'And decided I was so stupid and naive that you'd have a little fun with me.'

He turned her around to face him. 'And decided I was so stupid to have dressed that way that I should just go home.'

Finally, she looked up. He saw the tears in her eyes. 'Then why didn't you?' she whispered, anguished.

'Because after one look at you, I was a goner.'

'Would you two move up,' someone behind them whispered.

Harrison and Amanda closed the distance between her parents and themselves. He took a chance and reached for her hand. She resisted, but not as much as before. Maybe he was wearing her down.

'I fell for you the way a guy only falls once in a lifetime.'

'Please don't say things like that.' Amanda fumbled with her tiny pink silk purse, but she hadn't packed any tissues. Her heart felt as if it would burst.

Harrison quickly took his handkerchief and carefully blotted the tears trickling from her eyes. He was stricken. 'Don't cry. Just listen. I was trapped. I wanted you. I wanted to be with you every minute of the day. To dance with you. To hold you. To love you. I was scared to lose the geek persona.'

'Move up,' that voice behind them whispered.

Automatically, they followed the line. Amanda noticed that Marcy was looking at them, her eyes wide with surprise. In fact, Marcy was so startled that she wasn't shaking hands with the people directly in front of her.

'What about Marcy?' Amanda asked. She could hardly tolerate the thought of him in bed with her cousin.

'What about her? We dated about a month. Then I broke it off.'

Amanda whirled. 'You broke it off?'

He shrugged. 'Yeah. I couldn't take her attitude. She didn't understand why I wanted to, as she said, practically give away a virtual reality invention that could earn my company millions.'

That fit with Marcy's personality, Amanda thought sourly.

'But you understood immediately,' Harrison said, raising his hand to cup her cheek. 'That's when I knew that what I felt for you went beyond desire.'

'So did I,' Amanda whispered as much to herself as to him.

'You forgive me for pretending to be

someone I wasn't?'

Hope chased away the gloom from her expression. 'I suppose I will if you'll forgive me for the pine oil.'

He lowered his brows. 'I don't know. That was a lot worse than what I did.'

'Oh, you — you — geek!' Amanda cried softly. 'Don't press your luck. It's going to take a long time for me to get over thoughts of you and Marcy in bed.'

'Would thirty or forty years be time enough?' he asked, overwhelmed by the soft promise in her voice.

'It will take at least that long,' Amanda said. But she smiled.

Harrison grinned, nearly giddy with relief. It was going to be all right. Then his smile faded and he scowled. 'Wait a minute. What do you mean, me and Marcy in bed? That never happened!' he whispered.

'It didn't?' Amanda's voice was louder than she'd intended. 'Mom said that Aunt Gwen told her — ' she broke off. 'Whatever Aunt Gwen told her came from Marcy, I'm sure.' Speculatively, she eyed Harrison. 'You know, Nicole has an interesting theory about Marcy's popularity with men.'

'Let me guess.' He grinned. 'She's free with her favors?'

Amanda nodded.

'I wouldn't be a bit surprised. I can assure you, though, that my honor remained intact all the time we dated. The last time Marcy and I saw each other, I was trying to break it off, and she was trying to seduce me. And let me tell you, she doesn't take rejection very well. I never met a woman who knew so many cuss words.'

'Move up!' The voice no longer whispered, but commanded with loud irritation.

'So if your cousin didn't like you much before,' Harrison said, 'she's really not going to like you after we get married.'

'Married?' Amanda asked, whirling to face him.

'We need someplace private for this

talk,' Harrison muttered as Amanda looped her arms around his neck, smiling blissfully.

Then in front of Marcy, the groom, the family, and the rest of the world, Amanda pulled his head down and kissed Harrison as if she planned never to let him go.

15

'Tired?' Harrison asked, holding his front door open for Amanda.

'Yes, but too excited to sleep.' She yawned as if to put a lie to her words, then laughed. 'See how mixed up I am around you?'

'I hope you're not too tired from all that dancing at the reception to stay up a bit longer.'

'Gee, I don't know. A comfy bed kind of figures in my immediate plans.'

'Then we'll have to go someplace else. Mine reeks of pine oil.'

'Sorry about that.' Amanda grinned, not looking a bit sorry.

'Remind me never to make you really mad,' he said, chucking her under the chin.

'Okay,' Amanda said softly. 'Now, if you're real nice, you could sleep in my bed tonight.'

'You've got yourself a deal. But let's have dessert first.'

Amanda groaned. 'I couldn't eat another bite. I'll explode.'

'Here, darling, make yourself comfortable on the couch. Kick off your shoes. I'll be right back. This dessert is something special. You'll like it. I promise.'

Amanda willingly kicked off the satin high heel sandals and curled her legs under her on the couch.

'Close your eyes,' Harrison called.

Smiling, she did as he requested. The couch dipped as he settled next to her.

'Now, open them.'

Amanda opened her eyes. He held one of the biggest heart-shaped boxes of Valentine chocolates she'd ever seen.

'Oh, my. Where did you find this?' she asked, laughing delightedly. She took the huge box from him. In the middle of the lid was a silk-screened print of the Mona Lisa, bordered with gold lace.

'It took some doing, but I'm proud to

say you are the recipient of the largest, most impressive box of Valentine candy in the entire city of Houston.'

'Since you went to so much trouble, I guess I could manage to nibble on one of these bonbons.'

She lifted the lace-trimmed top away. In the very middle of the box, where the choicest chocolate should have been was a red velvet ring box, opened to reveal a huge, sparkling diamond solitaire.

Amanda hadn't thought the day could hold any more surprises. She'd been wrong. With her heart in her eyes, she looked at him.

Softly, Harrison asked, 'Be mine, Valentine?'

THE END

We do hope that you have enjoyed reading this large print book.

Did you know that all of our titles are available for purchase?

We publish a wide range of high quality large print books including:
Romances, Mysteries, Classics
General Fiction
Non Fiction and Westerns

Special interest titles available in large print are:
The Little Oxford Dictionary
Music Book, Song Book
Hymn Book, Service Book

Also available from us courtesy of Oxford University Press:
Young Readers' Dictionary
(large print edition)
Young Readers' Thesaurus
(large print edition)

For further information or a free brochure, please contact us at:
Ulverscroft Large Print Books Ltd.,
The Green, Bradgate Road, Anstey,
Leicester, LE7 7FU, England.
Tel: (00 44) **0116 236 4325**
Fax: (00 44) **0116 234 0205**

Other titles in the
Linford Romance Library:

A HEART DIVIDED

Sheila Holroyd

Life is hard for Anne and her father under Cromwell's harsh rule, which has reduced them from wealth to poverty. When tragedy strikes it looks as if there is no one she can turn to for help. With one friend fearing for his life and another apparently lost to her, a man she hates sees her as a way of fulfilling all his ambitions. Will she have to surrender to him or lose everything?

SAFE HARBOUR

Cara Cooper

When Adam Hawthorne with his sharp suit and devastating looks drives into the town of Seaport, Cassandra knows he's dangerous. Not only do his plans threaten to ruin her successful harbourside restaurant, but also Adam stirs painful memories she'd rather forget. When Cassandra's sister Ellie turns up, in trouble as usual, Cassandra needs all her considerable strength to cope. But will discovering dark secrets from Adam's past change Cassandra's future? And will he be her saviour or her downfall?

THE HAPPY HOSTAGE

Charles Stuart

When an agreement is made with the U.S.A. to build missile bases in Carmania, Elisabeth Renner and her friends plot to kidnap the American ambassador to Carmania and force the agreement to be cancelled. However, they get the wrong man: Charles Gresham, a budding British business tycoon. And he soon finds himself sympathising with his pretty captor. Then Elisabeth reluctantly decides to call it all off, and things really go wrong — when Charles doesn't want to be released!